Precious Memories Book 1,
the first 10 years

Little White Farm House in Iowa

A Fictionalized Biography of
Katherine Vastenhout

Carol Brands

ISBN: 978-1-4669-0349-4 (sc)
ISBN: 978-1-4669-0348-7 (e)

Trafford rev. 11/23/2011

 www.trafford.com

North America & International
toll-free: 1 888 232 4444 (USA & Canada)
phone: 250 383 6864 ♦ fax: 812 355 4082

*   *   *

**Written in Collaboration
with Katherine Vastenhout
by Carol Brands**

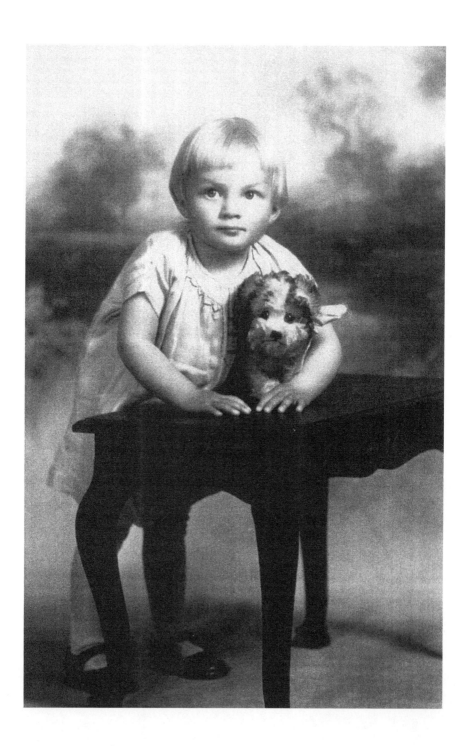

Precious Memories
By J. B. F. Wright

Precious memories, how they linger,
How they ever flood my soul!
In the stillness of the midnight,
Precious, sacred scenes unfold.

Precious memories, unseen angels
Sent from somewhere to my soul.
How they linger ever near me
And the sacred past unfold.

In the stillness of the midnight
Echoes from the past I hear:
Old time singing, gladness bringing
From that lovely land somewhere.

Precious memories, how they linger,
How they ever flood my soul!
In the stillness of the midnight,
Precious, sacred scenes unfold.

Precious memories, how they linger,
How they ever flood my soul!
In the stillness of the midnight,
Precious, sacred scenes unfold.

Precious father, loving mother,
Fly across the lonely years
And old home scenes of my childhood
In fond memory appear.

As I travel on life's pathway,
Know not what the years may hold,
As I ponder, hope grows fonder,
Precious memories flood my soul.

Precious memories, how they linger,
How they ever flood my soul!
In the stillness of the midnight,
Precious, sacred scenes unfold.

Precious memories, how they linger,
How they ever flood my soul!
In the stillness of the midnight,
Precious, sacred scenes unfold.

Preface by the Author

A year ago, Edgebrook Care Center—where I've worked now for eleven years—adopted a system called "Consistent Care". Each nurse's aide cares for twelve to fourteen residents rather than taking turns with all fifty-five residents. Day after day, five days per week, I work with the same residents. I feel like I have several dear mothers with whom I work daily.

One of these "mothers" is Katherine Vastenhout. Katherine moved into our care center on February 7 of 2007 at the age of 77. She is in Room 221 at the west end of my west hallway. I soon learned that mentally Katherine was 'way too young to be in a care center. Along with physical problems which brought her to Edgebrook, she suffered loneliness from young widowhood.

In our care center, the average age of residents is close to ninety years. Being younger than most residents, Katherine still maintains a host of interests. She has hundreds of valuable videos, often shared with residents. She plays her own organ in her room, to an audience of residents in the hallway. Outside her window hangs a bird feeder for her feathered friends. Her television is never on "soaps"—or even "game shows"—but on travelogues, history or human interest programs.

In daily conversations, I discover a lady with a life history of adventures. Her life shows what it was like to endure the Depression years as a farm girl in Iowa. These chapters need to be captured in print. When Katherine said the words, "My life should be put in a book," my heart responded, "Let's do it!"

As I write this, we are just beginning our collaboration. If things go as we hope, perhaps in a year a book shall be typed. Perhaps in two years the book shall be in print. If God blesses this new venture, perhaps, just perhaps, it shall happen. Let us begin . . .

Carol Brands, friend of Katherine, August, 2008

Dedication

I dedicate this book, first of all, to all of Katherine's relatives.
You have been on my mind in all of this writing. I have hoped that
Katherine's story would have permanent significance for you.
It belongs to you first of all.

I dedicate this book, secondly, to my family, my children.
You have heard me dream of having a completed book for years.
You have endured my incessant writing, of letters or poems or
stories. You have used my love for writing in having me critique
your own writing . . . until you became better writers than I am.
I look forward to possessing and reading your books someday.

I dedicate this book, thirdly, to my 90-year-old mother.
It is you, Mom, who taught me a love for reading and writing.
Your own history includes so many stories which I dream of writing.
I will, Mom; I will. Please live long enough for it to happen . . .
Better yet, come live in Minnesota to make it happen!
If God wills. If God wills.

And, finally, I dedicate this book to my husband of 35 years.
Your patience has made it possible to get this done, Harold.
How many times haven't you done dishes so that I could write?
Or started the beef roast for supper . . . because I was writing?
Or run errands for me? Or made phone calls? Or vacuumed?
Thanks more than I can say. I love you, Harold!

Above all, this book is dedicated to my God, Lord and Savior,
Jesus Christ. How I love Him, who "first loved me!"
Nothing happens without Him. He has been in every written thought.
May He prosper the writing. May it be to His praise.

Family Tree of Katherine Kroontje (Vastenhout)

Wilbur Kroontje—m. on February 16, 1927 to—Susie Tilstra
11/29/1899   10/26/1903

1. *Son* Wieba Jan (William or Willie) Kroontje 04/10/1928

2. *Daughter* Katherine Kroontje (Vastenhout) 06/03/1930

3. *Son* Gerrit Kroontje 05/22//1933

4. *Daughter* Dorothy Kroontje (Ricehill) 07/29/1934

5. *Stillborn Infant Son* 02/23/1936

6. *Son* John Cecil Kroontje 02/22/1941

7. *Son* Marvin Walter Kroontje 05/04/1942

Precious Memories:
Book 1. The First Ten Years

Little White Farmhouse by Rock Rapids

Table of Contents

"Lo, children are an heritage of the LORD, and the fruit of the womb is his reward."

Susie . . . hadn't anticipated the swift rise of the afternoon storm with its loud and multiple thunders.

Neither had the unborn baby within her expected the storm.

Chapter 1. June 2-3, 1930

Thunderstorm and Midnight Birth

Vroo-o-o-o-m! . . . Cra-a-a-c-k!

Accompanied by a long, thick, jagged streak of lightning, the loud clap of thunder shook the barn frame, causing its doors to rattle. The petite, dark-blonde, 26-year-old woman, on a low stool next to a feline, nearly upset her milk pail.

The young woman, Susie Kroontje, with her husband, Wilbur, was doing the daily, late-afternoon milking of the dozen cows which their farm boasted. She hadn't anticipated the swift rise of the afternoon storm with its loud and multiple thunders. After all, this was June 2, nearly summer.

Neither had the unborn baby within her expected the storm. The baby gave a sharp kick, making the woman grab her stomach, again nearly upsetting the milk pail. Her husband looked up in alarm.

"Are things okay there, Susie?" he questioned in his mild Dutch voice. Wilbur had been born and raised in the Netherlands and still spoke Dutch with Susie and close family. Susie, on the other hand, had been born in America and was fairly gifted in the American language.

"Ach, Wilbur, I think so. That clap of thunder caused this baby some alarm. It kicked . . . and for a minute there, it hurt, too. But it's over, I think . . ."

Just then another pain gripped her lower back, increasing in intensity as it built towards the front. The wife's face, normally rosy-cheeked, blanched as she gave a muted gasp. The husband again looked quickly at her, then questioned, "Do you think it is time, Susie? Has this storm started things?"

"I . . . I think . . . Maybe it will calm down if there is no more lightning, yes? Let me just sit for a minute."

"Okay, we'll wait. But no more milking, right? Try to relax."

The woman tried one more time to continue milking but found her fingers wouldn't work right. She moved the milk pail to a safe spot and sat on a hay bale, leaning against another bale to relax.

*　　*　　*

Although it made no sense—the rain and wind would soon undo it, anyway—the woman automatically straightened her long hair, which had escaped the bun into which it was pulled. She relaxed against the hay bales until another spasm of pain began to build, causing her to grit her teeth.

"Wilbur, I will run to the house and lie down, okay?"

"No, wait, Susie. I don't want you out in that storm alone. I have only two cows left to milk, then I will go in with you. If pains continue, I will drive to get the doctor."

"But, Wilbur, what shall we do with Willie? We can't leave him alone."

Wilbur's smile was tender as he glanced towards the calf pen where his two-year-old son was asleep. He had chosen the name of his first son, "Wieba Jan", after his own father, who still lived in the Netherlands. "Wieba" was "William" in English, although he was usually called "Willie".

But, uh, why was Willie in a calf pen?

The parents never dared to leave little Willie alone in the house while they milked cows. They were happy they had this clean calf pen where he could safely play near them. Usually he was content there. Today he had fallen asleep.

"Susie, since Wieba is sleeping, he won't be upset. Even if he wakens, he can't get out—and you know he wakes up slowly. I will be in the house only a few minutes, then I will take him with me. The neighbors have already agreed to take care of him.

"But I do *not* want you running through that storm alone, Susie. Wait five minutes and I can run with you so you can get to the house safely."

*   *   *

As she waited, Susie watched Wilbur work. She loved him so much! Her mind wandered back to their first meeting.

Susie had been to the fairgrounds in Rock Rapids with her parents, checking prizes they had won on produce. She had met Wilbur as he also looked over produce entries. Both of them had entered cabbages and tomatoes, so were in competition for prizes.

For Wilbur, it was instant attraction. He latched onto Susie and her family the rest of the evening. That led to courtship.

Another contraction, however, reminded Susie that courtship had long ago become marriage and she was soon to have her second child. She watched Wilbur hurry . . .

Yet five minutes became fifteen minutes before the last cow was safely milked and the milk put away. Wilbur blew out the barn kerosene lanterns and hung them on hooks. Chores were finished.

Another crack of thunder caused the last kerosene lantern to flicker dangerously despite its round glass protection.

Another contraction also gripped the woman. The message was clear: this was not a false alarm. The wild thunder storm may have started things . . . but started they certainly were.

She would need the doctor, today.

*   *   *

Wilbur Kroontje and Susie Tilstra had been married just three years and four months earlier on February 16, 1927. They had rented farmland eight miles northeast of Rock Rapids, Iowa—the first of their three rental farms—where they would live for roughly ten years. The farm was a typical quarter section, one-fourth of a square mile, adequate for a beginning farm.

1930 was the beginning of the Great Depression . . . but the industrious couple was intent on making a prosperous farm, working hard to build a herd of cows—to sell cream from milk as well as supply their own family needs.

The farm house was a typical farm house, if there is such a thing . . . although a very small home, just for a beginning family. It had no basement, just a small first floor and a still smaller attic. Outside the house, a crude stairway led down to a small cellar dug under the house.

Other than two porches, one enclosed and the other open, the main floor had only a moderate kitchen, a small dining room, and an even smaller bedroom. The upstairs attic room was a single room, later to be divided into two narrow halves, a girls' bedroom and a boys' bedroom.

Like most farm homes in 1930, the house had no indoor toilets, no plumbing, no electricity, and no telephones.

Because there were *no indoor toilets*, they used an old outhouse which in summer swarmed with flies. When in haste, they used a "chamber pot"—the fancy word for a pail with a lid.

Because they had *no plumbing*, water had to be carried in five-gallon pails from the windmill pump down the hill from the barn. Water for dishes or laundry was rain water; it was drained through a spout from the roof, through a charcoal filter, and into a cistern. They carried it in pails to wherever they needed it.

Because they had *no electricity*, they used gas or kerosene lamps. A Sears' Roebuck gas lamp, with an attractive white shade, hung from the ceiling in the kitchen. Kerosene lamps were to carry around the house, putting light wherever needed. These had to be closely watched when a storm caused the house to vibrate.

Because they had *no telephone*, there was only one way to contact a doctor: ride to town and get him.

*   *   *

The storm had not yet lessened. Wilbur left the last lantern hanging so it would not be dark if Wieba awoke before he got back.

Now he took over the safety concerns of his wife. He shielded her from wind and rain as they sloshed through growing puddles from barn to house. They had to skirt tree branches which had blown down.

Once in the house porch, Wilbur gave his wife a quick peck on the cheek and asked, "Can you get out of those clothes into something dry?" When Susie headed for their bedroom, he stripped off his own wet clothing, changing into dry clothes hanging on a hook.

Zipping his dry jacket, Wilbur headed for the bedroom. Willie's crib was just inside the door. Susie handed him Willie's coat, shoes and other clothes. They didn't own any suitcases.

Pausing as another contraction hit, Susie found her husband silently taking the boy's clothes into a box on the bed. Within minutes, he had left for the doctor.

*   *   *

In the early 1900's, babies in the Midwest were not born in the hospital. Only the wealthy would think of such a thing. Babies were born at home. Some poor families could not even afford a doctor. A midwife—a neighboring lady who knew what she was doing—would assist in labor. But most people were choosing doctors, and Susie felt fortunate.

Susie hated to wait for the doctor by herself, fearful of what could happen if the baby came before the doctor arrived. Since labor had just begun, she didn't think anything would happen that quickly. She *would* wait. She *must* wait.

To pass the time, she found things to do between contractions.

She made sure her already clean house was 100% spotless.

She checked the stew on the back center of the corn cob stove. Her husband would have supper warm when he returned.

She set out a large pan with water on the stove burner directly above the hot corn cobs, to be hot and ready if the doctor required it.

She laid a little kimono atop a baby's crocheted blanket in the baby crib which Willie had used two years earlier. Now the new baby would have that crib

But what a relief when she heard the sound of the Model T Ford returning! What a relief when the door opened, wind nearly blowing in the doctor . . . who struggled to shut the door while Wilbur brought the Model T out of the thunderstorm to the garage.

What a relief also to find that while neighbors were taking care of Willie, the neighbor's wife had come along to assist the doctor as a midwife. From then on, all Susie had to do was crawl into bed. Doctor and midwife took over.

*   *   *

The storm continued to howl. Lightning continued to zigzag, rain to pelt the windows, and thunder to cause vibrations of the buildings. The contractions also never let up. It approached midnight as the mother gave birth.

Midnight! The father, pacing outside the bedroom, heard the first wail of the newborn baby. Instantly, he glanced at the clock. *Exactly* midnight: not one second earlier or later.

But if the baby was born at *exactly* midnight, on which day was it born? Was it born on June 2 or on June 3? The father scratched his head in indecision. He decided to leave that up to Susie.

Susie smiled a tired smile when asked to choose the day.

"June 3," she whispered. "Our baby was born on June 3. Now tell me: is it a boy or a girl?"

Leaning over to check, a broad smile crossed Wilbur's face. The baby was a girl, a tiny, precious, six pound girl. The farmer's big hands stroked the baby's almost invisible blond wisps of hair. Looking to his wife, he asked, "Susie, what shall we name her?"

The answer came quickly.

"Katherine. Katherine Kroontje. After my mother, Kate Tilstra. Is this not a pretty name?"

The name sounded perfect to Wilbur. Willie had been named by him after his father. This child was named by Susie after her mother. The father was elated that the baby was healthy and well.

*   *   *

Looking at the baby's tiny size, he wondered if she would fit inside his new shoebox. Going to the porch, he found the box, picked up a soft flannel blanket to line it, and gently placed the baby inside.

The shoebox was a perfect fit. It became Katherine's first tiny crib.

Now the doctor had to be taken care of. The doctor's usual fee was $25 but he was satisfied to receive that value in farm produce, too.

Leaving to bring the doctor home, Wilbur paused in the doorway to watch the baby begin her first feeding. It always seemed like a miracle how a baby instinctively rooted to find its mother's milk.

All was well with Wilbur's world and he was thankful. He might be only a farmer, struggling to make a success of his first farm. It might be thundering outside . . . but he was a rich man.

He had a wonderful wife, a fine son . . . and an adorable daughter.

What more could a man want?

"Give us this day our daily bread . . ."

This stove from the SEARS' catalogue was similar
to the stove of the Kroontjes. Two main differences:
the Kroontjes' stove had an open shelf on the top,
no door in front of it as this one had.
And the Kroontjes' color was not black but ivory.

Chapter 2. Fall 1931 Part 1

"Please Take Care of Kat'rin"

"Lord, thank you for this food. For Jesus' sake, Amen."

As the noon meal ended, 3½-year-old Willie prayed in Dutch the memorized prayer, then pushed back the high stool on which he sat, ready to run and play. He raised his eyes to Wilbur.

"May I go now, Papa?" he dutifully asked. When Wilbur nodded permission, he scooted his chair back and headed for the dining room.

At the doorway he stopped again.

"May Kat'rin play with me?" he asked. Mama had recently bought him a set of blocks to play with. Besides teaching the alphabet, they were fun to stack and to arrange into houses or pens or other shapes.

This time Mama nodded permission. She was already wiping jelly off of Katherine's face and unlatching the tray of the wooden high chair. It would be good to have the two children busy while she did dishes and began baking bread.

*   *   *

"Where will you be this afternoon, Wilbur?" Susie asked.

"Right in the yard," Wilbur responded in Dutch. "I have several things to finish before I pick corn."

"Good!" Susie responded, meanwhile busy clearing the table. "I've been thinking we should run to Rock Rapids for some groceries. Would today work?"

Wilbur scratched his head while he thought.

"I think that in three hours I could use a break," he answered. "How does that work for you?"

"I can have bread ready to raise in about an hour," Susie answered. "It takes two hours to raise and bake. Meanwhile, I could fix a stew for supper . . .

"Yes, in three hours I can be ready. Shall we plan on it?"

"Works for me," replied Wilbur. "If you need me for anything, I'll first be cutting lawn with the field rake and after that be mending fences."

"Perfect!" Susie answered. "I'll have coffee ready for you before we leave, and a rhubarb jelly sandwich with fresh bread, yes?"

Wilbur's eyes lit with anticipation as he nodded, grabbed his hat and headed out the doorway to the barn for the horse mower. Pulled by the horse, the mower was used both to cut grass and hay.

*   *   *

Susie's dishpan was also her mixing bowl for bread ingredients. She quickly got out Oxydol, her dish detergent. With fingers flying, in fifteen minutes dishes were finished, the dishpan rinsed and ready for making bread.

Susie baked bread everyday so she needed no recipe. She could make variations of her basic recipe without hesitating. She could substitute butter for oil, use different flours, even substitute milk for water to add flavour.

Mixing enough for two loaves of bread, Susie kneaded the dough, rolled it into a large ball in the dishpan, covered it with a dish towel and set it on the warm reservoir of the stove to raise. She loved the smell of yeasty dough, knowing the entire family loved homemade bread.

*   *   *

Susie was just placing the dough on the stove's water reservoir to raise when she heard a little noise. Glancing around, she saw nothing at first . . . then spied a small toe peeking out from the left side of the stove.

"Katherine, are you in the kitchen?" she exclaimed. She had been so busy and Katherine so silent that she hadn't heard her enter the kitchen.

"Ma-ma," Katherine said. She peaked around the side of the stove.

To understand what happens next, you must understand this stove.

Susie's stove was a recent model from the *Sears, Roebuck & Co.* catalogue. From the front, it had a foot-square drawer to the top left and another drawer beneath it. Into the top drawer would be placed corn cobs to burn, the most efficient source of fuel on the farm.

Cobs were presoaked in kerosene to make them burn efficiently. Once they were burning, more cobs would be added, not kerosene-soaked.

As the burning cobs produced ashes, these filtered down into the ash bin drawer below it. A rod was attached to the stove to stir the cobs to make the ashes filter down. Every few days the ash bin needed emptying. Corn cobs needed replacing as soon as they finished burning.

Behind the stove, where toddler Katherine was, stood a galvanized aluminum box to hold unused corncobs. The top of the box was open so that a bushel of cobs could be dumped into it. Below the corn cobs was a cubby hole with sliding doors, just large enough to hold a metal pail.

Here was danger! Inside the metal pail was kerosene. Cobs were placed into the kerosene to soak. These were "starter" cobs, ready to burn well in the stove. The sliding doors kept the kerosene smell out of the kitchen.

Susie immediately saw that little Katherine had managed to open the sliding doors to the kerosene pail. Kerosene-soaked cobs were scattered on the floor. The child *had* been into the kerosene cobs. What if . . . ?

Quickly Susie grabbed the toddler and sniffed. She sucked in her breath in horror because there was no doubt. The smell was overwhelming. Katherine had either sucked the cobs or drunk the kerosene!

*　　*　　*

Panicked, Susie grabbed Katherine and ran towards the dining room. "Willie! How long has Katherine been out here?" she called. But Willie, alphabet blocks ignored, was by the window watching Wilbur cut the lawn grass. He hadn't noticed Katherine leave. Willie was so entranced by Wilbur that he scarcely heard Mama. Susie dashed out the door, carrying Katherine with her.

Wilbur looked up in surprise as Susie flew into the yard carrying Katherine. "Whoa!" he called to the horses, stopping the cutter.

"Wilbur!" gasped Susie. "I . . . I didn't see Katherine enter the kitchen . . . and I think she has been drinking kerosene. The smell is so strong. We must get her to the doctor instantly, Wilbur."

Wilbur moved fast. Susie had scarcely finished before Wilbur was off the horses, unhitching the cutter, leading the horses to the barn. "Get the children into our Model T. I will crank it. Quickly! Don't clean up. We'll go as we are."

*　　*　　*

The Model T was older than their marriage but Susie still didn't want grease all over it; she grabbed two old sheets in the house to protect its seats. As she reached for the sheets, the kerosene odor on Katherine almost made her gag; so she also grabbed a little dress for Katherine and a paper bag for the dirty clothes. Seeing her purse, she instinctively grabbed it as well.

Holding the sheets, the dress, the bag, the purse, and Katherine in one arm, and holding Willie's hand with the other, she bolted back out of the house, dragging the wide-eyed boy with her.

"Wait one second, Willie," she commanded as she set the children on the ground. She covered the front seat with one sheet and the back seat with another.

"Now, Willie, into the back seat," she directed, holding the door for him to slide in. It was a good thing Willie was obedient; time was critical.

By this time Wilbur had the Model T cranked up and ready to go. Susie held 1½-year-old Katherine. The automobile lurched backward as Wilbur backed out of the garage, then forward as Wilbur shifted and headed for the gravel road.

*　　*　　*

Between lurches of the automobile, Susie changed Katherine's clothes. She put the kerosene-smelly clothes into the bag, shoving the bag under the seat.

The Kroontjes lived eight miles northeast of Rock Rapids. At thirty miles per hour—the fastest they could go—the drive took sixteen minutes. Although the doctor sometimes did home visits, they had no phone to call him. They hoped he would be at his home office in town, able to see Katherine immediately.

Susie kept sniffing Katherine. Even with clothing changed, the smell was overwhelming. How much kerosene had the child drunk? Katherine became drowsy even though they were just starting on a bouncy ride down gravel roads.

Willie, on the other hand, was very much alert and excited.

"Where we go, Mama?" he exclaimed eagerly, bouncing up and down in excitement. His eyes were glued to the scenery outside the car, taking in every tree, every mailbox, every side road they passed. "To Wock Wapids? Why?"

Susie informed Willy that Katherine had drunk kerosene and that they needed the doctor.

The boy's eyes widened a bit in fear. "Will Kat'rin be sick?" he asked.

"She could be very sick," Susie answered, wondering how much she should tell the boy. She didn't want to make him fearful but had to say enough so he would understand.

"Villie," Wilbur—with his Dutch brogue—spoke from the left, although very loudly to speak over the noise of the Model T engine, "ve aren' sure how much Kat'erine drank, okay? Ve hope nod doo much."

Wilbur paused. Although he usually tried to speak American with the children, his brogue made it difficult. "Ve mus' pray, Son. Can you pray?"

Willie obediently bowed his head and folded his hands. He prayed the words out loud. "Father in heaven, please take care of Kat'rin. She is my sister, God, whom you gave me. Make her all better. Amen!"

Glancing at Wilbur, he remembered another lesson about prayer. He bowed his head again. "If it is your will, God."

Peaking through his fingers, he saw Mama, nodded his head, and added, "For Jesus' sake. And . . . thank you!"

"*Be anxious for nothing . . . but pray . . .*"

The tiger lily in this chapter represents the faith of a child and hope in God, our only help.

Chapter 3. Fall 1931, Part II

"Turning Blue!"

Who can underestimate a child's faith? A child's prayer?

Having prayed about Katherine, Willie promptly forgot her plight and concentrated on the unexpected outing. He watched dust spurting into the roadway behind them and orange tiger lilies sprouting from ditches. It seemed only seconds until they crossed the bridge over Little Rock River and lurched madly into Rock Rapids.

By this time, Susie was desperate. Katherine's lethargy had increased. Susie shook the child, panting, "Faster, Wilbur! She's turning blue!"

"I can go no faster, Susie," Wilbur said in Dutch from the front seat, giving the Model-T every bit of gas he could. "But we are nearly there. At least we have this vehicle instead of horse and buggy. Here is town now . . . and there is Dr. Corcran's office . . ."

*   *   *

As Wilbur slammed on the brakes, the Model-T jerked to an unceremonious stop, throwing them all forward even as they grabbed on tightly.

Almost before the automobile stopped, Wilbur was out the front door and to Susie's door, reaching for Katherine and running into the doctor's home office. Normally he would have helped everyone . . . but this was an emergency.

Now that they had arrived, Susie became almost paralyzed with fear. Moving slowly, she took Willie's hand and followed Wilbur into the building.

The door to the doctor's office was also the door to his home. The front rooms of the main floor had been made into his office. Wilbur had already disappeared from the front waiting area into the doctor's back room before Susie and Willie entered the door.

A few other patients were sitting on winged chairs in the waiting room. Behind a desk sat a young receptionist. Smiling at Susie, she said, "Could you please take a seat, Mrs. Kroontje? The doctor is with Katherine right now."

Susie wanted to rush back with Katherine but knew she could not leave Willie. Nodding to the receptionist, she found a seat next to Willie. A colored magazine helped to keep Willie occupied—one of the few national magazines of the 1930s, the *National Geographic*, with exotic pictures to enthrall the reader.

*   *   *

After what seemed an interminable length of time, the receptionist called them to the back room. Susie, glancing at the clock, saw that it had only been fifteen minutes yet. Taking Willie's hand, she walked with quick grace, her head high although her heart quivered.

They followed the nurse into the back room, finding Wilbur on a chair with Katherine on his lap. Katherine still looked groggy but her skin color was less blue and she was smiling at the doctor. The doctor let her play with his stethoscope, a shiny and exciting toy. Willie, fascinated, stared at the stethoscope until the doctor let him hold it, too.

"Susie, let Doctor tell you what he told me," Wilbur said.

"Certainly. Doctor?"

"Mrs. Kroontje, I didn't do much. Katherine began to breathe normally the minute your husband took her back here. All I did was to give her orange juice to dilute what she swallowed.

"Be thankful! Katherine didn't drink enough kerosene to be lethal. Then she might not have made it into town. You were wise to take her in so quickly."

"Doctor," Susie interrupted, "Can there still be side effects?"

"Yes, Mrs. Kroontje. She could have pain because kerosene could irritate the intestines or the stomach. She could throw up. She could have mental wandering. Sometimes people have the opposite reaction and are hyperactive.

"We don't know all possible side effects. Keep a close eye on her. If nothing happens today or tomorrow, then you can relax."

Susie whispered, "How can we make sure this doesn't happen again?"

The doctor smiled warmly. He appreciated the question.

"Children, as you saw today, move quickly. You can't watch too closely!

"I'm not sure what you can do about the kerosene in your cob box. Of course, close the sliding doors. But a two-year-old might still open them. I guess just never leave your children unattended near the stove."

Wilbur asked the next question. "Doctor, if such a thing should happen again, should we do anything differently?"

Dr. Corcran pulled out of a file drawer a sheet of typed paper. "I'll give you the standard list of guidelines which we physicians are given.

- *"Do not induce vomiting.* This can cause the patient to get kerosene into the lungs, where it can do much more damage.

- *"Make her drink*—while conscious. Drinking will dilute the kerosene. It doesn't really matter what you drink, just drink.

- *"Change clothing*—if any kerosene is on it. Spills on the clothing will cause extra breathing of the toxin.

You were wise, Mrs. Kroontje, to put the clothes into a bag while in the car.

"I doubt this will be repeated. I've never seen it happen twice in one family. Once is enough! Everyone watches so it doesn't happen again."

*   *   *

Mr. Kroontje extended his hand to the doctor.

"Thank you so much, Doctor Corcran. We won't let it happen again. Our children are God's gifts and we love them."

"Mr. Kroontje," the doctor said quietly, "don't beat yourself up about this. Accidents happen. Some are careless but some can't be helped.

"Just thank God that He reminded you of what is most important in life. You still have your child to raise. I expect to see these two children have their own children before I retire."

Tears rose in Susie's eyes at the doctor's kind and wise words. "Thank you, Doctor. We do thank God for our children. We will do our best."

*   *   *

Leaving the doctor, the practical side of the Kroontjes took over. Since they had needed a trip to town anyway, this was it. They still had their stained and wrinkly work clothes on—but they would do for today.

Wilbur took Willie's hand. They headed for the hardware store and the government post office. From the hardware store, Wilbur needed a few tools. From the post office, which had just recently separated from the hardware store, he was hoping a plow might have arrived from *Sears, Roebuck & Company.*

Meanwhile, Susie carried Katherine into the grocery store, then set her in a chair . . . carefully in her line of view. The friendly storekeeper gave Katherine a sucker to keep her occupied.

Susie had not intended to sew clothes but right now wanted nothing more than a new dress for her little girl. She looked over several dress patterns and chose a little-girl pattern with a tie in the front, embroidery below the tie, and lace at the hemline. Looking over materials, she chose a baby blue color with white polka dots on it. She added delicate baby lace for edging.

Then Susie quickly tried to recall all the things she needed. They had left so quickly that she had no list with her. She stood still for a moment, thinking through each kitchen cupboard. As she lined everything up on the countertop, she was quite sure she hadn't missed anything important.

The grocery store owner had just placed everything into a large box when Wilbur returned. He carried the box while Susie helped Katherine.

*   *   *

The return trip home was not quite so fast. Susie calculated the math. Sixteen minutes to get to town. Thirty minutes at the doctor's office. Thirty minutes in the stores. Twenty-five minutes to return home. Over two hours in all . . .

Oh . . . the bread! Would it still be okay?

The moment the Model T stopped, Susie jumped out and rushed to the kitchen. Normally, heat from cooking would make the dough raise quickly but this time the kitchen was cooler and the dough was perfectly raised. Relieved, Susie ran back out to inform Wilbur and to collect Katherine and Willie. She was delighted when Wilbur showed her one of his purchases: a gate to screw across the dining room doorway. What a help that would be!

For now, the children were tired. Susie put them to bed for a late nap. She and Wilbur had a quick cup of coffee with homemade cookies. Then Wilbur did milking chores while Susie rushed to get supper ready.

It was too late to make a stew but Susie was able to heat some home canned beef with fresh potatoes and late green beans from the garden. With home canned, chunky applesauce alongside and milk to drink, it would be a fine meal.

* * *

The children were awake by the time chores were finished and the meal ready. They bowed their heads while the father prayed in Dutch.

"Father in heaven, thanks for sparing Katherine's life today . . ."

This could have been the end of Katherine's story!

> *"Wisdom is the principal thing; therefore, get wisdom."*

Birth of the T

1893
Henry Ford builds his first working engine.

1896
Henry Ford drives his first "quadricycle," in Detroit.

1903
Ford Motor Company incorporated and Model A runabout sold.

1904 to '07
Seven other models launched; Model N is forerunner of Model T.

1908
Model T debuts as 1909 model; experiments with rope-and-pulley factory system will lead to mass-production, moving assembly line.

1913
Model T is first car assembled on moving assembly line; annual output doubles to 168,220 cars.

1915
More than half a million Fords built.

1916
Production savings reduce price of runabout to $345.

1922
Price of Model T touring car dips to $298.

1924
Ten millionth Ford built.

1927
Final production year for Model T.

This photo of a 1925 Ford Model T is taken from the July 2008 REMINISCE magazine. The list of significant FORD dates is from the same source. Used by permission.

Chapter 4. Spring 1935

Papa Buys Something Expensive

Papa was behaving strangely. Willie noticed first. Katherine noticed, too.

Every time Papa had to do something with the Model T Ford, he acted upset. Last week, Mama had needed some things from town. Papa said that he didn't have time to be running to town so often. His work wouldn't get done!

That was strange . . . because Papa never argued about going to town before. If Mama needed him to go to town, he might wait a day or two but then would go. He enjoyed visiting friends in town.

Today Mama was looking through the SEARS' catalogue. She commented that she would like to order school clothes for Willie and Katherine from the catalogue, since catalogue clothes were strong and inexpensive.

Papa never argued with Mama's purchases because Mama was careful with spending. But today Papa shot Mama a glum look and responded that if she could order whatever she wanted, he should be able to do the same.

Then Papa said added under his breath, "You'd think a man could buy whatever he chooses, long as he has the money. But no, a man's wife thinks she has to make all the decisions."

What was Papa talking about? Why was he so angry with Mama?

Mama hadn't answered Papa in front of the children. She had merely raised her eyebrows to indicate that the children were listening.

* * *

There were now four children in the family. Willie was nearly seven years old, Katherine nearly five years old. A son, Gerrit, would be two years old next month. And the fourth child was a girl named Dorothy, nine months old.

Papa and Mama often said that each child was a blessing. Willie and Katherine believed it, too. Katherine adored her younger brother and sister.

While Mama put Gerrit and Dorothy to bed—both in cribs in her bedroom downstairs—Katherine cleared the table. She was too young to wash dishes in hot soapy water. Mama washed dishes while Katherine dried them.

With chores and dishes finished, Willie and Katherine played Tic Tac Toe using the light of a kerosene lamp. Usually this was a peaceful time of day.

* * *

Today, as usual, Mama sat on the porch with mending in her hands. Papa had an open catalogue in his hands and leaned close to Mama. Mama shook her head while Papa talked and gestured. He was trying to prove something to Mama.

Occasionally Willie and Katherine could hear a word or two. They heard Papa say, "I know it's a Depression . . ." but then couldn't hear the rest of the sentence. They heard, "Sure you work hard, Susie, but so do I. When you wanted a new stove . . ." and the words became fuzzy again. Then they heard two whole sentences: "Remember when the babies were born? Remember how long it took to get the doctor when the car wouldn't start? Well . . ."

Trying to hear was what Mama called "eavesdropping".

"Willie," Katherine whispered, "what is wrong?"

Willie shrugged. "Papa wants to buy something. Mama doesn't approve."

"Is it something expensive?" asked Katherine.

Again Willie shrugged. "If it is, it must be important. Papa never wastes money. I'm sure they are trying to figure out if it is worth the money."

"Is the Depression still going on?" asked Katherine. She had only lived during the Depression and wasn't sure what life was like not in a depression.

"Yes, it is, but Papa and Mama raise almost all their own food, so, any money they earn selling things, they can spend. They give to the church and they help a widow lady in town. So they do have a little money to spend . . .

"They just don't tell us everything."

*   *   *

A few days later, it seemed that Papa and Mama had resolved the problem. Mama seemed quiet, maybe worried as well. But Papa was happier, whistling or singing as he worked. When Mama again mentioned buying clothes for school, he cheerfully agreed, "I would enjoy seeing Katherine in boughten dresses."

That evening after Gerrit and Dorothy were in bed, Mama sat by the kerosene lamp with a *Sears' Roebuck* catalogue and wrote out an order. She carefully inserted a check into the envelope with the order. From her purse she extracted a roll of stamps, carefully licking one three cent stamp. Then she walked to their country mailbox, inserted the envelope and put the red flag up.

Papa met her as she returned from the mailbox. He gave her a hug. Now Willie and Katherine knew for sure that the problem was solved.

But they didn't know what the problem had been. It was a mystery. Would they ever know?

*   *   *

It was early morning in late April. Willie and Papa were finishing chores before Willie left for school. Papa seemed extremely cheerful, whistling under his breath. Pausing, he commented to Willie, "Do you know who is the greatest man of this century?"

Willie shook his head. He didn't know.

Papa continued, "The greatest man is Henry Ford. No doubt about it. Can you guess why?"

Willie hesitated. "Because he invented the assembly line?"

"No," Papa replied, "Mr. Olds did that. Henry Ford just improved the assembly line with his Model T, starting in 1913.

"Henry Ford is the greatest man *because he made the automobile affordable for the common person.* Did you know that the word 'affordable' comes from Ford's name? Automobiles made by other companies are so expensive only the rich can afford to buy them. Mr. Ford tried to keep cost at less than $400 so anyone could afford one. The Model T which I bought before our marriage was $298 . . . brand new!

"Because it was affordable, the Model T outsold every other automobile. Do you know how many Model Ts were sold? Fifteen million! That's a lot of vehicles, Willie!"

Willie nodded. Fifteen million was a big number.

"From the start of using the assembly line in 1913, Mr. Ford never changed the Model T Ford. He kept it the same until 1927. By then the competition had so many improvements that Mr. Ford knew he'd have to make changes, too. He shut down operations for two years to set up for his new Model A Ford. The new Model A is a little more expensive but still affordable."

"How is the A different from our T, Papa?" asked Willie

"The new Model A Ford is a different car!" Papa answered. "Among other changes, it has a complete car top, no open sides. The rain can sweep or the winds howl . . . children are secure inside. A woman won't get her hair messed.

"Another great change is that you don't have to crank up the car on the outside anymore. A man can simply get inside the car and turn a key, fancy that! The car cranks itself to start!

"And all this, my boy," Papa finished, smiling broadly, "at prices the average John Doe can afford. This man here, though fighting finances daily, can afford it. Henry Ford is the common person's hero!"

* * *

Now Willie and Katherine guessed what Papa and Mama had been discussing. They didn't know any details but still tingled with excitement. The family was getting very cramped in the Model T Ford. Besides, it was getting old. Papa wasn't happy when he had to take days off his farm work to get the Ford repaired. A new vehicle would be wonderful.

Could Papa afford it . . . even though Mr. Ford made it affordable?

*   *   *

Willie went to school Mondays through Fridays.

Today was Saturday. Saturday was Willie's day for extra chores. He did before-school chores every day, of course. But on Saturday he did all sorts of other farm chores as well. Then Papa could get extra work done.

So it was a surprise to him when Papa cheerfully announced, "Get yourself cleaned up, Boy. We are going to town this morning."

"Really, Papa? Just you and I?"

"Nope, the whole family is going. We are going to have a surprise. We'll leave when everyone's ready."

Mama already had breakfast on the table. The two babies were in their places. Everyone sat down to a quick yet hearty breakfast of oatmeal, eggs, bacon and milk. Papa did not omit devotions but read a Psalm and closed in prayer.

Devotions made Katherine feel secure, having God's blessing on the day. Mama hurriedly stacked dishes in the dishpan and washed them. She did *not* want to come home to stuck-on egg and grease! Katherine dried the dishes, doing a pretty good job for a four-year-old girl. She didn't drop even one cup.

"Good job!" Mama praised her. "What would I do without my helper?"

Katherine shyly dipped her head. Praise made her happy but embarrassed.

*   *   *

Usually when they went to town, Mama headed for the general store to get groceries and whatever else she needed. Papa headed for the hardware store where the men would sit and talk while having coffee.

Today, Papa passed up the general store and the hardware store and continued to a lot at the end of the street. This lot had been purchased awhile back as a new automobile lot. Papa couldn't imagine how a man could make a living when he sold only one item. Could he sell a car every day?

There, sitting smack in the middle of the lot, was a brand new Model A Ford. It was sparkling clean and shiny.

"Look, Willie," Katherine whispered. "The color is dark green!" All Model Ts were black. Papa had said Mr. Ford preferred black.

As Papa's Model T chugged to a stop, the owner of the automobile lot rushed out of his home. He hurried straight to Papa with a huge smile on his face, holding out his hand in greeting. Papa pumped his hand back, looking very pleased with himself.

"Ah, the whole family is here, aye?" the salesman asked, then reached around and shook hands with each of them, including Katherine and the little tots. Baby Dorothy even chortled for him, which amused everyone.

"Willie, what do you think you are here for?" asked the salesman. He was eye to eye with Willie as he asked.

"I . . . I don't really know, Sir," replied Willie. He was hoping so much it hurt but didn't dare to say what he thought.

"What about you, Little Sister?" the salesman asked Katherine. But Katherine was too shy to answer. Only her shining eyes spoke volumes. She, too, hoped!

"Well, Children, I'll let your papa show you why he is here," the salesman said. "I have in my hands the keys to your father's latest purchase.

"It's a wise purchase, Mr. Kroontje. Everything is made of the strongest materials so it should hold up.

"It's a beauty. You're taking good care of your family."

*   *   *

Katherine, remembering the earlier dissension between her parents, glanced at Mama. But Mama, too, looked pleased. She held Baby Dorothy as all six of them walked towards the new, dark green vehicle on the car lot.

"Susie, Dear, here is our new Model A Ford," Papa formally said as they reached the automobile. "It is a vehicle large enough to hold this growing family. And we can get to church all in one piece, without weather damage."

Papa opened Mama's door, helping her and Baby Dorothy into the passenger seat. Mama never did learn to drive an automobile, not even in later years when they had automatic transmission. She was afraid to drive. Driving was the man's role, she thought.

With Mama and Dorothy safely inside, Papa opened the back doors for the children. Unable to wait, Willie scooted in first, all the way to the window on the opposite end. Katherine was shorter and had to lift her skirt to get in. Two-year-old Gerrit sat in the middle between them, holding Katherine's hand.

Papa didn't get in right away. He first went to the house with the owner and wrote him a check for the cost of the car. It was more than $400 but still a lot cheaper than any other car would have been. He never told the children the cost.

*   *   *

Once Papa got back, he didn't turn to go back to the stores. He got the car started and the entire family went for a ride in the country. They had to make sure that Model A Ford was keeping its promises!

And it did. Although Papa needed practice with the clutch, and although it sometimes "backfired", the Model A rode as smoothly as any vehicle they had ever seen. Papa was ecstatic. Mama was happy.

Katherine and Willie stayed glued to their windows. They could hardly believe that they could ride inside a vehicle without wind ruffling their hair. It seemed too good to be true.

*   *   *

None of them knew how soon this Model A Ford would be of great value to the family. How could they know that it would actually help to save a family suffering from the Depression? That would come later.

"Ask, and it shall be given you . . ."

Chapter 5. July 1935

Vagrant Visitors

Katherine shimmied up the trunk of her favorite tree. It was early afternoon and all the forenoon chores were finished. Mama had just given her a few unusual hours of freedom.

The early July sun was shimmering hot. The coolness of the big cottonwood tree felt wonderful to five-year-old Katherine. She loved the cottonwood tree and the anonymity it offered her. In its cool, spacious depths she felt lost to the world.

Katherine's short legs found it difficult to shimmy up very high. But she so wanted to feel completely alone! She struggled to climb until she found a perch high up in the tree.

Peeking through the leaves from this branch, she could see 'way out over the farm. To her left, she could see the small house. Straight ahead, she could see the barn, the slope to the river, the meadows across the river, and—far in the distance—the bridge at the end of the farm. She could see the dirt road, which was a straight road, crossing twice over the meandering river. The first bridge over the river was closer so it looked much larger than the distant bridge.

What a wonderful spot to relax! Katherine was so relaxed that her eyes began to close. Still peering out from half-closed eyes, she was startled when in the distance, beyond the second bridge, she saw unexpected movement.

It looked like . . . no, it was . . . a horse!

It looked like . . . yes, it was . . . a second horse! A third!

The horses were pulling wagons. Very colorful wagons, Katherine thought. But, quite old wagons with the colors faded. Three wagons, three horses. What on earth . . . ?

On each wagon a man sat, directing the horse which pulled the wagon. As the wagons came nearer, Katherine could hear the men calling to the horses. "Whoa, Char-lee . . . Whoa there. We gonna stop now, Char-lee. Whoa-a . . ."

To Katherine's surprise, the man pulling the first wagon turned his horse right down their driveway. The other two horses followed. All three horses and wagons came to a stop in the large yard, between the house and the barn.

Not wanting to be seen, Katherine sat very still. The tree was a safe place to see without being seen.

*   *   *

Katherine knew who the visitors were. At least she thought she knew. She had heard Mama talking about them on Sunday.

"There are Gypsies wandering these parts right now," she had heard Mama say to Father. "They were south of Sioux Center last week. They stop wherever they want, expecting handouts. What do we do if they come here?"

"Now, Susie, don't borrow trouble," Papa had calmly replied. "You know those Gypsies wander around, needing help to feed their families. We as Christians need to help the poor."

"Well, the Bible also says we are to work!" Susie had snapped back. "People aren't supposed to go around just looking for handouts from other hard-working people without lifting a finger themselves. Who do they think they are?"

"God makes people different from each other, too, though," answered Papa. "We have a Dutch tradition of hard work. I'm kind of proud of that. But other people don't know how to change their lifestyle. Gypsies can't change their ways anymore than our brown dog can change its color to purple.

"I've seen their children, Susie. Those poor kids are sticks and bones. When they come here, I'd sure like to help those skinny kids have a good meal or two. Just think of the kids."

Watching the three wagons stop in the yard, Katherine peered closely through the leaves to see the Gypsy children. Were they skinny sticks and bones?

*   *   *

The children stayed hidden inside the wagons. They were just as scared as Katherine. Katherine could hear the Gypsy mamas talking rapidly to the children. They must have told them to stay in the wagons and not make any trouble.

But the Gypsy mothers soon appeared. They pushed aside the curtain doorways to the wagons. The mama in the first wagon was first to step out. She wore a long, boldly colorful, but rather old dress. Over her arm, she held a large basket of woven reds and yellows. She walked quickly up to the house.

Katherine was afraid. She could hear Mama's words: "You stay away from those Gypsies, hear? Gypsies steal children!"

Gypsies didn't seem to have any fear. The lady knocked boldly on the door. When Mama opened the door, the lady pushed her way right inside the house. Katherine, peering through the tree leaves, could see her looking this way and that. Katherine remembered Mama saying that Gypsies were thieves. She wondered what the lady could steal from their house.

At least Baby Dorothy was asleep in the dining room. The Gypsy lady couldn't see her. She couldn't steal her.

*   *   *

Katherine saw Mama come out of house with the lady. She could hear them talking. Curious, she began climbing down the tree. She was afraid . . . but curiosity was stronger.

"I will give you a hen," Katherine heard Mama say. "We have big white hens. If you cook one, it will make a large pot of soup for your family. I will give you some vegetables to put in the soup. I will give you a second hen, too. The second hen will lay eggs for you."

To Katherine's surprise, the lady didn't look happy. She exclaimed, "A white hen! Ach, no! The devil is in white hens!"

Then Katherine noticed Papa and Willie standing in the barn doorway. They had heard the commotion and come outside to see what was going on. Willie was hiding behind Papa but had his hand over his mouth, laughing at the idea that the devil was in the white hen.

The Gypsy man left the wagon and walked over to Papa. Katherine quickly slid the last four feet to the ground and ran towards Mama. She wanted to hear everything!

Mama was still trying to convince the Gypsy lady to take two white hens. "Madam," said Mama, "you need food for your children. You take this white hen. It is called a Leghorn Chicken. It is not so fat but it lays many eggs. You can have eggs all summer if you take this egg-laying hen."

"No, no!" exclaimed the Gypsy mama, not understanding the value of the eggs. "De devil am in white chick'ns! I no like de devil! I want de colorful chickens. De colorful chick'ns am nice 'n fat. 'N colors keep away de devil!"

Katherine wondered, "Is that was why Gypsies have so many colors on their clothes and wagons? Do they think colors keep them safe from the devil?"

* * *

Mama scratched her head in defeat.

"Well, then," she said, "I'll ask my husband."

Wilbur and the Gypsy father walked over to Mama. Willie tailed Papa. Katherine tailed Mama. A Gypsy girl peaked through curtains on the wagon.

"I think you'd be better off with white hens. Then you'd have eggs all summer," Papa said agreeably. "But if you're afraid of them, I'll give you the Road Island Reds. You wait here while I catch them."

"Want to help me, Willie?" he asked. Willie promptly jumped the fence and they began the hot task of chasing the hens.

* * *

Katherine and Mama were entranced watching Papa and Willie chasing the red hens. Each of them was holding up a colored hen in triumph . . . when Mama noticed the Gypsy lady slipping back inside the house. Alarmed, she immediately charged toward the door. Katherine followed.

The Gypsy lady had already gone through the porch and into the kitchen. As Katherine entered the kitchen, she saw the Gypsy lady in the small dining room next to the kitchen. She had found Dorothy's crib, where Dorothy was now awake and cooing happily. The Gypsy lady clapped her hands in delight. She held out her arms for Dorothy to come. Dorothy, always happy and friendly, lifted her arms to the lady.

But Mama was terrified. She had heard stories of Gypsies stealing children . . . and she believed them. Alarmed, she rushed forward and pushed the Gypsy lady aside.

"No! No!" she exclaimed. "You may have chickens, but not children! This is *my* baby girl! You leave her alone!"

Now the Gypsy woman looked angry. She glared at Mama. "I just like to hold white baby," she answered hotly. "I no steal. I no steal nothin'. I take what you give, no more."

Then, head held high, she stalked from the house and back to the wagon.

The men had finished. The two Road Island Reds were tied inside the wagon. The woman, still glaring back towards Mama, climbed into the back. The Gypsy man, smiling towards Papa, climbed into the driver's seat, picked up the reins, and clucked to the skinny horses. Down the driveway they went.

*   *   *

"Papa," Katherine asked a few days later, "who are the Gypsies? Are they Indians? Where are they from?"

Papa had also been doing some scouting.

"Well, Katherine, Gypsies aren't Indians. At least, not American Indians. In a way, they are Indians, though . . ."

"Apparently, there were groups of Indians from the real India who were migrants, wandering peoples. These people were very musical and gifted. They would travel from place to place and entertain, make some income, then move on.

"These people moved westward from the real India. They eventually moved to Europe. In the 1800s, groups of them moved to the Americas. These are the groups we see."

"But they didn't entertain us, Papa," Katherine commented. "How do these Gypsies earn a living?"

"I'm not sure about the ones who came here," Papa answered. "I've heard, though, that some of them get jobs at fairs doing hand tricks or stunts with animals. Some of them sing and dance. Some tell fortunes."

"Oh!" exclaimed Katherine. "The Gypsy lady wanted to tell Mama's fortune. Mama wouldn't let her. Was she trying to pay for the chickens?"

Papa grinned. "If so, it didn't work, did it? Mama wants nothing to do with fortune telling. As far as Mama is concerned, the Gypsies simply demanded Free food.

"And that is what Gypsies do when there is no work for them. Then they roam the countryside, whenever the weather is warm enough. They may try to entertain to pay, but if the entertainment is refused, they simply ask for handouts.

"At night, they stop by some secluded park and make a little feast. If you would pass them there, you would see them having a party, singing and maybe dancing as they eat."

*　　*　　*

Papa couldn't shake Mama's fear of the Gypsies. She remained positive that the Gypsy lady had intended to steal Dorothy. Over and over, she warned her children to stay away from the Gypsies. She did *not* want to lose her children.

But all Katherine could remember were the hollow eyes of the little Gypsy girl who had looked out of the wagon. While she felt afraid of the Gypsy mama, she felt sorry for the girl.

"Mama," she whispered, "Gypsies are even poorer than we are. We work hard. But they have nothing. Not even food. That little girl was so skinny . . .

"Mama, I'm glad Papa and you know how to work. I am so, so glad that we have enough food. And I hope that our chickens helped that little girl have two good meals!"

"Now abideth faith, hope, charity, these three:
But the greatest of these is charity."

Chapter 6. August, 1935, Part 1

Mama's Tears

Standing with their ears pressed against the stairway wall, five-year-old Katherine and seven-year-old Willie listened to the sounds inside their parents' bedroom. Their mouths hung open as they stared at each other, eyes wide with confusion.

There was no doubt about it. Mama Susie was crying!

Mama was a strong lady. She didn't usually cry at all. When she did cry, she usually cried silently, tears squeezing out of her eyes while she silently wiped them away. In Katherine's five years of living, she had never heard her mother cry like this. Willie and she had heard the cries upstairs in bed, which was why they had gotten up and sneaked down the stairs together.

Wilbur was in the room with his wife. His deep voice was soothingly calm. Willie and Katherine pressed their ears close to the wall but could not make out what he was saying. They would have to wait to find out what was wrong.

*　　*　　*

Back upstairs where they were supposed to be sleeping, Willie and Katherine sat on the landing between their bedrooms. Willie shared the bedroom on the left with their younger brother, Gerrit. Gerrit was two years old and slept in the boys' crib. Katherine had the corn husk mattress in the bedroom to the right. Dorothy still slept in the baby crib downstairs.

"Willie, what is wrong?" Katherine whispered.

Willie whispered back, "I think it has something to do with a letter they received. Did you see the mail today?"

Katherine shook her head no. She was only five years old and didn't pay much attention to the mail. She couldn't read yet. Willie, two years older, was going into second grade. He could read . . . and he often ran to the mailbox to get the mail.

"There was a letter from North Dakota in the mail today. I think it was from Uncle Will and Aunt Ann Kroontje. Do you remember hearing Papa talk about them?"

This time Katherine nodded her head. She always listened closely to conversations between her parents and had several times heard them tell stories about Uncle Will and Aunt Ann. She knew that father adored his older brother, whose American name sounded like his own. She knew that Uncle Will and Aunt Ann had two children who were teenagers, named Willie—just like Brother Willie—and Tillie. Willie and Tillie. The names said together sounded silly.

"I remember Papa and Mama talking together once. They were talking about the . . . the . . . Depress . . ."

"Depression," responded Willie, sounding important because he knew the word. "They were talking about how our country is in a depression and many people are losing farms and homes. Depression means things are bad and there isn't enough money. That is why we have to work so hard to keep our farm and have enough food. We have to raise all our own food because of the Depression and we have to be very careful with finances. The President of the United States can't figure out how to stop the Depression.

"In the letter a month ago, it sounded like Uncle Will and Aunt Ann were having a hard time. The Depression is bad up there in North Dakota. They can't make a profit. They hardly have enough to eat. They may lose their farm. They are almost wishing they had never come to America but had stayed in the Netherlands. It was bad there but so far it is worse here."

"So what will they do?" asked Katherine seriously, studying Willie's eyes. "Will they go back to the Netherlands? Is that why Mama is crying and Papa has red eyes, too?"

"No," Willie said, shaking his head emphatically. "They won't go back across the ocean. Things were too bad there all the time. They are hoping that in a few years this depression will end. But they aren't sure they can make it that long. It is very hard for them."

"So what do you think the letter says?" asked Katherine. "Why would it make Mama cry?"

"I don't know," Willie admitted, looking worried. "I guess we'll just have to wait until they tell us. We'll ask them in the morning, okay?"

"Will they tell us?" replied Katherine. "They won't always tell us things."

"I know," answered Willie. "But we'll keep asking. I guess now we'd better get some sleep, yes? Before they hear us talking and come up here?"

*   *   *

"Willie! Katherine! Time for chores!"

Farm days in Iowa in the 1930s began early in the morning. It was only 5:00 A.M. and still dark outside when Willie and Katherine were awakened by the morning call.

It didn't take much to make the two get up quickly. They still remembered their mother's tears the evening before. Besides that, usually their father called them and this time it was Mama calling them. And outside, they were hearing unusual noises.

Hurriedly pulling on their farm clothes, Willy and Katherine nearly collided as they met on the small landing outside their bedroom doors. Both were very sober and wide awake, wondering what they would learn today. But neither said a word. They just hurried downstairs.

Mother was waiting for them with pails for their morning chores. "Willie, you go get the cobs from the pig yard. Katherine, you gather the eggs. Meet me in the barn where I will be helping your father milk the cows. Right now he is checking out if the Model A Ford is well oiled and running well. We'll have breakfast after chores are finished."

That was strange. Why was Papa checking out the automobile now, instead of doing the chores? Looking at each other sideways, Willy and Katherine each knew what the other was thinking: it had to have something to do with that letter.

Not needing to be told again, each of them reached for his pail and headed outside to do the chores.

*   *   *

Willie thought it was fun to get the corn cobs from the pig yard. He would first give the pigs their morning feed, scattering slop and ear corn on one side of the pig yard. "Slop" was a mixture of skimmed milk and ground up corn or oats. Willie enjoyed shouting at the pigs and making them run while he picked up as many cobs as he could from the other side of the yard. As soon as the pigs began returning, wondering if he had more feed for them, Willie would shout and chase them away again.

Each time his pail was full of cobs, Willie dumped it into the bushel basket outside the fence. As soon as the bushel basket was full, his chore was finished. The full basket was too heavy for him to carry. Papa would take the basket into the house and dump the cobs into the metal cob bin behind the stove.

Katherine did *not* think it was fun to get the eggs. She had to go into the fairly dark hen house and feel around in the straw to find the eggs. The good part was that each hen usually laid her eggs in her own nest. The bad part was that she might still be in her nest and not want to get out.

Sometimes Katherine had to chase a hen out of her nest with a stick. A few times she had gotten good scratches from angry hens. Mama would have to put iodine on the scratches so they wouldn't get infected. Iodine hurt!

There was one hen which defied all the rules and laid her eggs wherever she felt like it. Katherine would always have to hunt for her egg. She would begin by checking her nest, but it was seldom there. Then she would check wherever she saw a bit of straw. Today it took her ten minutes to find the egg. It wasn't in straw at all but in a corner of the dimly lighted henhouse. She had to rub manure off it before she could put it into her basket. At least, she thought, it was a nice large egg.

By the time Willie and Katherine had finished chores, Papa had the Model A back into the small garage and was in the barn helping Mama with the milking. As Katherine entered with the eggs, she caught a few words they were saying. It sounded like "Herreid", "North Dakota," and "Washington". Katherine was sure they were talking about Uncle Will and Aunt Ann because they lived in North Dakota. But she couldn't guess why they would talk about Washington.

Mama looked up from the cow she was milking. "Katherine, take your egg basket into the kitchen. Careful, now! We don't want any eggs broken. Clean your hands off and go check on Gerrit and Dorothy. Understand?"

Katherine carefully picked up her basket of eggs again. Slowly, she walked back out the door. She wanted to stay and listen to what they were saying but knew better than to argue.

Willie was big enough to help with the barn chores so he stayed outside. Careful not to spill any milk, he carried the nearly full buckets of raw milk to the milk separator on the porch. After breakfast, Mama would use the separator to separate cream from raw milk. The family liked to drink raw milk with cream in it. The plain cream would be sold in town. The skim milk which was left would feed the hogs and cats.

*   *   *

Katherine found Dorothy still sleeping in her crib. Gerrit was awake and singing songs to himself. Katherine was proud to help Gerrit up and to the boys' chamber pot. She helped Gerrit dress himself and climb into his high chair.

There was still no sound from Dorothy. Mama came in at last. She was pleased to see Gerrit in his high chair. She scurried around getting oatmeal and milk on the table. In a few more minutes, Papa came in and led in opening prayer. Mama quickly fried eggs while everyone ate the oatmeal.

Everything seemed busy. Papa seemed busy. Mama always seemed busy, even as she quickly ate.

But to Willie and Katherine, everything was going slowly. They had only one thought: would they learn what was wrong last night? Why had Mama been so upset?

"(If) I have not charity, I am nothing."

"Papa always read reverently but today there was an extra depth to his reading, as though he wanted the children to hear his thoughts."

15 If the foot shall say, Because I am not the hand, I am not of the body; is it therefore not of the body?

16 And if the ear shall say, Because I am not the eye, I am not of the body; is it therefore not of the body?

17 If the whole body *were* an eye, where *were* the hearing? If the whole *were* hearing, where *were* the smelling?

18 But now hath God set the members every one of them in the body, as it hath pleased him.

19 And if they were all one member, where *were* the body?

20 But now *are they* many members, yet but one body.

21 And the eye cannot say unto the hand, I have no need of thee: nor again the head to the feet, I have no need of you.

22 Nay, much more those members of the body, which seem to be more feeble, are necessary:

23 And those *members* of the body, which we think to be less honourable, upon these we bestow more abundant honour; and our uncomely *parts* have more abundant comeliness.

24 For our comely *parts* have no need: but God hath tempered the body together, having given more abundant honour to that *part* which lacked:

25 That there should be no schism in the body; but *that* the members should have the same care one for another.

26 And whether one member suffer, all the members suffer with it; or one member be honoured, all the members rejoice with it.

27 Now ye are the body of Christ, and members in particular.

28 And God hath set some in the church, first apostles, secondarily prophets, thirdly teachers, after that miracles, then gifts of healings, helps, governments, diversities of tongues.

29 *Are* all apostles? *are* all prophets? *are* all teachers? *are* all workers of miracles?

30 Have all the gifts of healing? do all speak with tongues? do all interpret?

31 But covet earnestly the best gifts: and yet show I unto you a more excellent way.

CHAPTER 13

THOUGH I speak with the tongues of men and of angels, and have not charity, I am become *as* sounding brass, or a tinkling cymbal.

2 And though I have the *gift of* prophecy, and understand all mysteries, and all knowledge; and though I have all faith, so that I could remove mountains, and have not charity, I am nothing.

3 And though I bestow all my goods to feed *the poor,* and, though I give my body to be burned, and have not charity, it profiteth me nothing.

4 Charity suffereth long, *and* is kind; charity envieth not; charity vaunteth not itself, is not puffed up,

5 Doth not behave itself unseemly, seeketh not her own, is not easily provoked, thinketh no evil;

6 Rejoiceth not in iniquity, but rejoiceth in the truth;

7 Beareth all things, believeth all things, hopeth all things, endureth all things.

8 Charity never faileth: but whether *there* be prophecies, they shall fail; whether *there* be tongues, they shall cease; whether *there* be knowledge, it shall vanish away.

9 For we know in part, and we prophesy in part.

10 But when that which is perfect is come, then that which is in part shall be done away.

11 When I was a child, I spake as a child, I understood as a child, I thought as a child: but when I became a man, I put away childish things.

12 For now we see through a glass, darkly; but then face to face: now I know in part; but then shall I know even as also I am known.

13 And now abideth faith, hope, charity, these three; but the greatest of these *is* charity.

CHAPTER 14

FOLLOW AFTER charity, and desire spiritual *gifts,* but rather that ye may prophesy.

2 For he that speaketh in an *unknown* tongue speaketh not unto men, but unto God: for no man understandeth *him;* howbeit in the spirit he speaketh mysteries.

3 But he that prophesieth speaketh unto men *to* edification, and exhortation, and comfort.

4 He that speaketh in an *unknown* tongue edifieth himself; but he that prophesieth edifieth the church.

5 I would that ye all spake with tongues, but rather that ye prophesied: for greater *is* he that prophesieth than he that speaketh with tongues, except he interpret, that the church may receive edifying.

6 Now, brethren, if I come unto you speaking with tongues, what shall I profit you, except I shall speak to you either by revelation, or by knowledge, or by prophesying, or by doctrine?

7 And even things without life giving sound, whether pipe or harp, except they give a distinction in the sounds, how shall it be known what is piped or harped?

8 For if the trumpet give an uncertain sound, who shall prepare himself to the battle?

9 So likewise ye, except ye utter by the

Chapter 7. August, 1935, Part II

A Plan of Brotherly Love

The entire time they ate, Willie and Katherine tried to keep their eyes on their food but every so often glanced at each other with questioning eyes. When would Papa and Mama say something? Surely something was afoot . . .

The meal was eaten with the usual banter between parents. Then Mama cleared off the dishes and set on coffee for Papa and her; the children were given a cookie and a glass of milk.

While Papa's coffee cooled, he took down his Dutch Bible and read a chapter. He read out of order for he normally read straight through the Bible and right then was reading in *Genesis*. The children had been enjoying the stories of Joseph so wondered why he now read from *First Corinthians*, the 13th chapter. But they listened as Papa stressed certain verses:

> *"Though I have all faith, so that I could move mountains,*
>   *and have not charity, I am nothing.*
> *"Though I give all my goods to feed the poor,*
>   *and have not charity, I am nothing.*
> *"Charity endures long, and is kind . . .*

> *seeketh not her own profit . . .*
> *"Now abideth faith, hope, charity, these three:*
> *but the greatest of these is charity."*

Papa always read reverently but today there was an extra depth to his reading, as though he wanted the children to hear his thoughts.

*   *   *

Usually when he finished reading, Papa went straight into his closing prayer. Tonight, he began to talk, looking at Willie, then Katherine, then Gerrit, as he talked. Mama tried to keep baby Dorothy quiet so he could talk without interruption.

"Children, yesterday your mother and I received a letter from Aunt Ann Kroontje in North Dakota. You have never met her because Uncle Will and she are too poor to travel and live so far away. It is a long trip to go see them. Because of the Depression, because money is so scarce, we have never felt we could travel to them, either. But we have kept in touch through letters.

"As you may know from hearing us talk, your Uncle Will and Aunt Ann have been especially hard hit by the Depression. Both South and North Dakota have had very dry weather so that crops are almost impossible to raise. The price of animals is so low that some people have been killing their animals; feed is too expensive and there is no profit in selling them.

"I guess you are too young to understand all that but you are not too young to understand that people can be very poor for many reasons."

Papa paused to make sure they were all listening.

"In the letter we received yesterday, your aunt was describing how difficult life is right now. People are leaving the Dakotas by the thousands. If Will and Ann don't do something quickly, they will lose everything.

"Will and I have a brother named John, your Uncle John Kroontje, who lives in Washington. Mama, do you have the world globe? Show the children where Washington is."

After Mama got the globe, Papa pointed to North America. He showed how the central part of North America was the United States where they lived. He pointed to the upper left corner, right next to the Pacific Ocean, to the state called Washington.

For the cousins to get to Uncle John in Washington, they must go west through Montana and Idaho. There were *no* good paved roads, not even one. They would travel by train.

Next Papa showed where they lived in Iowa. To get to Herreid, they must cross a little bit of Iowa and about half of South Dakota. The cousins lived in North Dakota, just above central South Dakota.

Uncle Willie and Aunt Ann had moved to North Dakota from the Netherlands because of the cheap land prices plus the railroad, father explained. They didn't have much money and there were very few people living out there. They thought that with the Missouri River nearby, there should be water resources. Plus the government had built a railroad west of the Missouri River; which made it easy for them to move there as well as made a way to ship animals to markets.

They moved there along with other Dutch people, who formed the towns of The Hague and Zeeland, North Dakota. Uncle John had moved there with them, but a few years back he had sold his farm and moved to Washington.

The lack of water was a surprise. The water in the Missouri River had not reached their farm. There was no irrigation system to bring the river's water to them. When there was rain during the World War I years, they had been able to survive. But during the Depression years, their farm was a dust bowl.

The dryness was so bad that the Dakotas had what were called "Black Blizzards". God was speaking, the minister once said, telling people that He alone was in control of the weather and they must pray to Him for rain and all their needs.

*   *   *

"Papa," Katherine asked, "why don't Uncle Will and Aunt Ann move here? We have almost enough rain, don't we?"

"A good question, Katherine," Papa said quietly. "We haven't had enough rain, either, but we've had enough to give us small crops. Your mother and I wrote them a few months ago to suggest that they move here.

"But it took all their money to buy the farm they have right now and they have no money to start over again. They are nearly destitute. Destitute means they hardly have enough food and clothes and have no money. No one wants to buy their farm when it won't produce enough for a living."

"What can we do, Papa?" asked Willie soberly.

"There isn't a lot that we can do, Willie," Papa said soberly. "We are just getting started ourselves. Our house is too small to have them live with us. Certainly, we would do that if it saved their lives. We even offered that.

"But let's get back to Uncle John. Uncle John moved to Washington, where there are also other Dutch settlers. There is enough water up there. There is also land which is reasonably priced. It is a good place to live.

"Although Uncle Will cannot afford to buy a farm, Uncle John has found a farm for them to rent. He will help them start a new dairy farm. That's what brothers are for, isn't it?"

"When will they move, Papa?" asked Willie.

"Will they move before they starve?" asked Katherine at the same time.

Papa was glad they asked good questions. He smiled.

"They would move today if they could but they first have to sell what they have, even if they don't get a good profit. They also want to harvest what they have, even if it is a small crop. They need to make arrangements to take what they have by train. They are trying not to butcher their cows so they have a small dairy herd to start over with in Washington.

"In the meantime, since last year's crop is all used up, they don't have any meat to eat. Your question was good, Katherine.

"Your mother and I discussed this last night and decided that we could help them a little right now. We want to visit them again before they move, anyway. It may be the last time we ever see them.

"Our visit could be a way to help them survive until they can move. We will take along for them anything we can spare until our own harvest."

"What sort of things will we take them, Papa?" asked Katherine eagerly. "Can we take them potatoes? Our new potatoes are starting to come in now, although they are still small and we want them to get bigger. And we have an apple tree which is starting to get ripe. Can we bring them apples?"

Willie was a little older and understood economics better.

"Papa," he said thoughtfully, "you said that you might butcher our extra chickens because they are eating so much and we can't sell them at a profit. You were even thinking of butchering some pigs. Can any of this help them?"

Papa looked surprised that they thought so well.

"Your mother and I were discussing the same things last night," he responded. "It is true that we are thinking of killing the extra pigs after we butcher for ourselves. We can't afford the price of the feed right now nor can we sell them for profit. And we can only eat so much ourselves.

"But neither do we have any way to get this meat to Uncle Will and Aunt Ann. It is such a hot, long trip that the meat would spoil. And how could we take the pigs to them alive? We can't think of a way to do this.

"However, we think we could maybe take them some chickens. We could pack them in a crate and tie the crate onto the automobile. It will be a noisy trip but, if you can stand the noise, we could take some hens to them.

"Along with the chickens, we'll pack enough food inside the car to feed ourselves and maybe leave a little extra for them."

*   *   *

Willie and Katherine both caught the word "you".

Katherine squealed, "Papa! Are we all going to go up there? Willie and me and Gerrit and Dorothy? All of us?"

Papa and Mama both smiled at their excitement.

"Of course, Children," Mama answered the question this time. "Did you think for just one moment that we would make such a trip and leave you behind? We will go as a family!"

"As a family," Katherine echoed contently.

"When do we leave?" asked Willie, the practical one.

"The sooner the better," replied Papa seriously. "They need the food right now. As soon as the car is ready, clothes are washed and packed, and the chores are lined up, we will leave. The biggest thing is to get someone to take over our chores while we are gone. He has to know exactly what to do. We think that we can be ready by next week Monday."

Mama added, "Katherine, we ordered three dresses for you to start school. Willie, you have two good bib overalls coming. They should arrive yet this week. You can use them also for this trip. The two babies will have to wear what they already have. Their clothes are hand-me-downs, not new, but they will do."

"Now," Papa finished, "we had better start some action. But let us first ask our heavenly Father to bless our plans."

Everyone closed their eyes while Papa prayed. Katherine knew that their plan was a plan of love which would meet the approval of their heavenly Father.

She couldn't wait to see the cousins whom she had never met.

> # *"Covet earnestly the best gifts."*

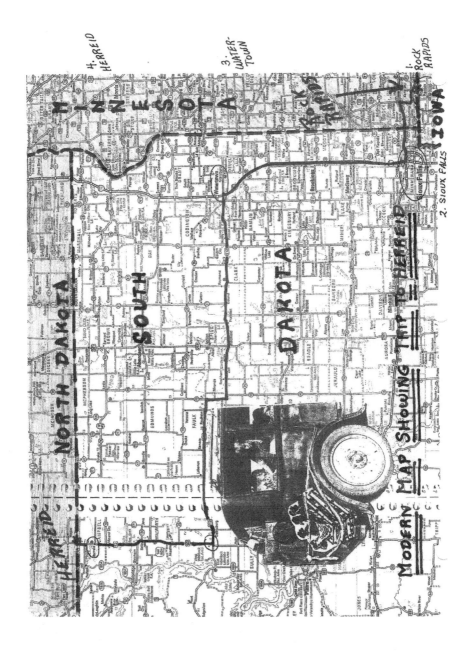

61

Chapter 8. August, 1935 Part III

Long Trip in the Model A Ford

It was velvety dark outside.

Rubbing the sleep from her eyes, Katherine responded to the voice of her mother calling her. She couldn't yet tell time but she knew it didn't seem like time to get up yet. There was no moonlight or even stars, it seemed.

But Mama's voice was insistent. "Katherine! Are you up? We must leave on the trip in one hour."

Then Mama's hand was on Katherine's shoulder, gently shaking her. Katherine could not ignore Mama's hand. She sat up, blinking sleepily. "Is it morning already, Mama?"

"No, Child, but we must get up to leave. You can go back to sleep once we are on the way to North Dakota. Now we must get chores done so we don't have to pay anyone to do them this morning.

"Quickly, pull on your farm clothes and go get the eggs. Take your bath and get ready to leave while I make breakfast. All in one hour. Rise and shine!"

*   *   *

Now Katherine's brain woke up. Today was trip day!

Pulling on her chores' dress, she ran down the stairs in haste. On the porch were lined up everyone's shoes. Willie was already putting his shoes on, heading out the door. Katherine was mere seconds behind him.

She had not thought about how different her chores would be that morning. Papa was in the hen house before she was, carrying a large wire crate with a top that could be latched shut.

Ah, yes! They were to take along hens for Uncle Will and Aunt Ann. Papa had to get them into a crate for the trip. It made Katherine's chores easier because, once Papa caught the hens, it was easy to pick eggs out of empty nests.

Papa packed the crate just enough so the crate was as full as possible while leaving enough room for the birds to move a little. They must not suffocate.

The younger, tastier hens could provide meals for Uncle Will's family until they left their farm for Washington. The older hens would lay eggs for them, one egg per day until the hens were eaten the last week.

Katherine was happy that the "ornery hen" was one of those Papa packed. Now she wouldn't always have to hunt every corner of the hen house for its egg.

The squawking of the birds was already deafening. Katherine wondered whether she could stand that sound for the entire trip to North Dakota.

Katherine tucked the eggs into a box and padded them with straw. These eggs would be tomorrow's breakfast in Herreid. She would guard them under her seat so they wouldn't get broken.

*   *   *

Back in the house, Katherine hurried with her bath. Papa milked alone today while Mama got the babies ready and supervised everyone's bath.

Before he did chores, Willie had drawn water from the stove's reservoir and poured it into the round galvanized tub near the stove. He had also gone outside to get more water and put it into the reservoir to get warm again.

Mama's own bath was finished before she even woke up the children. Now, while the children took baths, she scurried about serving breakfast and packing lunch for the trip. She already had suitcases sitting by the door for Papa to pack into the Model A. All the hurrying was exciting, thought Katherine.

Mama had the round galvanized tub with bath water set near the stove so she could supervise baths at the same time as she put on breakfast. When Katherine tested the water with her toe and found it too cold, Mama added a little hot water from the tea kettle.

"Hurry!" Mama admonished. "Don't let the water get cold for Willie!"

Willie was still helping Papa outside but, as soon as Katherine was finished, Mama went to the door and called him. While Katherine dressed upstairs, he took his bath. When Papa was back in, they ate together.

Papa prayed like always, except he added a prayer for their journey.

The breakfast was an easy one, just oatmeal and milk with honey. Mama gave everyone an extra large helping because she said they must not get hungry too quickly. The trip would take long enough without stopping too often to eat.

Mama had a huge picnic basket prepared to take along, with sandwiches that would not spoil too quickly.

The sun was just peeking over the tops of the trees across the river when everyone loaded into the Model A Ford and Papa turned the key to start it up. As soon as the motor had a steady sound, he lifted the clutch, the automobile jerked into life and they roared off.

Katherine clutched the seat to keep from jerking off. Mama held onto one-year-old Dorothy. Two-year-old Gerrit was snug between Willie and Katherine in the back seat. The whole family was there. Katherine was content.

*   *   *

The roads Papa took were easy for Katherine to memorize. The first country road had the number "1". Who couldn't remember that? Road 1 turned north onto Road 75. While all of the roads were dirt roads and could get muddy in rainy weather, right now there was no mud, only dust. Highway 75 wasn't as dusty as the country roads. But it went up and down over several hills.

In about half an hour they turned west on Road 90, which was not tar, either—tar roads were rare then—but was a well packed and much wider road. It took nearly two hours to get to Sioux Falls. By then Katherine was starting to get sore from all the bouncing around in the car.

"Are we almost there?" she shouted over the noisy engine.

Mama looked amused. "Child, look over there," she said, pointing to the east. The sun was just above the level of the trees. Papa's large watch said 7:30. "Do you see the sun? Katherine, the sun must go all the way up in the sky, must cross way to the other side of the sky, and must disappear behind the trees in the west. It will be dark again before we get there."

"Really?" shouted Katherine. "It will take the whole, whole day?"

"Quit shouting, Katherine," Willie shouted at her. "Papa and Mama told us that last week. You knew it would take all day to get there."

"But all day is so l-o-n-g!" responded Katherine.

"Well, but all day it is. Now hush, Child! Didn't you want more sleep?"

Yes, she was tired. Within minutes, Katherine's eyes closed and she fell back asleep. Gerrit and Dorothy and she all slept the morning away. They slept away all of Road 29. Even Willie slept a little while.

By the time they woke up again, it was noon. They were in Watertown. Papa had stopped at a filling station to get gas before they again turned west.

*   *   *

"Road 1, west . . . Road 75, north . . . Road 90, west again . . . Road 29, north again . . . Road 212, west . . ." Katherine chanted softly to herself. She wanted to memorize all the roads they took. She would surprise Papa on the way home by saying which road came next.

Road 212, going west from Watertown up to Road 83 just past Gettysburg, was a straight road. It was important because it divided South Dakota . . . but still, it was a very dusty road.

Anyone could tell that Road 212 had not seen rain in a long time. So much dust billowed from their automobile that, when they met another automobile, both of them had to slow down to a crawl to make sure they didn't collide. The dust was a thick fog around the vehicles.

It was easy to figure out that crops couldn't grow well out here. How could crops grow in hot dust? Katherine could figure that out even though Papa hadn't told her.

About every three hours, Papa stopped for gas. Each time, Mama quickly shooed the children into rest rooms and gave them a little something to eat. They would have fun pumping and squirting water from the pumps for a drink.

"Don't drink too much, Children!" Mama warned them. "We can't stop along the way for rest stops, hear?"

Each gas stop took thirty minutes if they hurried, more if they dawdled.

With each stop, they also gave water and feed to the hens in the wire box. The hens would become quiet while the automobile was in motion because they were too scared to squawk while flying along at thirty miles per hour. But the moment the Model A slowed down, their squawking would resume. They were telling the whole world that they *did not* like traveling and they *did* need water!

But they quit squawking as soon as the water was there for them.

The sun was already low in the sky when the family turned north on Road 83. Soon the sun was gone, the sky dark with no stars. Katherine asked, "Are we there now? Now it is dark!" But Mama told her they still had a long ways to go.

Katherine was almost asleep again when Willie shouted, "There it is! That sign says 'Herreid: population 600'! Are we there?"

Shouting over the roar of the Model T, Papa replied, "We're nearly there now, Willie. Herreid is the last town before we get to Will and Ann. However, we are still in South Dakota. Watch for a sign that says, 'North Dakota.' Then we follow the little map Uncle Will sent us to his house."

Sure enough, in another ten minutes they saw a crude sign welcoming them to North Dakota. Following Uncle Will's road map, it took only another five minutes until they found a modest house tucked back from the road by some box elder trees.

"Are we there now, Mama?" exclaimed Katherine.

And Mama, smiling as the Model A came to a jerking halt, said as she nodded, "Yes, Katherine, we have arrived. Here come your two cousins.

"Jump down and say Hello."

* * *

But Katherine could not bring herself to say anything. As her two cousins came running, she could only stare. She had thought they were poor in Rock Rapids but they did not look anything like these cousins. These cousins were so skinny! Their faces were pinched. And their clothes, though neatly patched and patched again, were threadbare and too small for them.

She forgot her grief, however, in the excitement of the cousins as they reached them. They may have been hungry for good food but were even more hungry for family contact. They were so isolated up in North Dakota!

They ran with outstretched arms.

Katherine found herself welcomed with a huge hug from Cousin Tillie. Still hugging Tillie, she found herself enveloped in a much bigger hug from Auntie Ann . . . and then from Uncle Will.

Never had Katherine felt more loved.

*　*　*

The squawking of the hens ended all the hugging.

Mama was the first to come to her senses and break away from the emotional reunion. Though still wiping tears from her eyes, she exclaimed, "Oh my! We must take care of those poor chickens before they die of thirst. Have you any water, Will and Ann, for these hungry and thirsty critters?"

Uncle Will promptly turned to the two boys. "Willie," he said to his Willie, "while we get this chicken crate down, go pump some water."

Everyone was so thirsty by then that the two girls followed the boys. They were careful not to waste the precious water but still stuck their tongues out for slurps of water as it came out of the pump. It tasted a bit gritty because it came out of parched ground but it was still water. Every drop was a treasure.

*　*　*

Later on, Katherine couldn't remember a great deal of the two days they spent with the cousins.

She remembered laughter as they enjoyed the dried beef sandwiches Mama Susie had packed in abundance to take along . . . and how Aunt Ann stopped her family from eating too much lest they become sick; their stomachs weren't used to rich protein anymore.

She remembered sleeping on a couch, Willie on the opposite end. The couch was protected with a horsehide robe. It was hard to sleep on that rough, prickly horsehide.

She remembered a special treat that Auntie Ann provided. A grocer had given it to her and she had saved it for them. She gave each of the children a heart shaped lollipop with cute little rings in the inside. You had to lick the lollipop almost gone before you could get the rings.

Once she had the ring, Katherine ran to the pump to wash it off. She kept it on her finger for weeks. It was her memento of Auntie Ann.

She remembered that after their short visit, she thought the cousins looked healthier and happier. Everyone felt so glad that they had been able to have this one last visit before they would be separated by six states.

What surprised Katherine was the feeling of dread that began to lodge in her own soul. The cousins, living through the worst of this Depression, had seemed to accept the awfulness of their situation.

But she was not able to accept it . . . not then or ever. The dreadfulness of the dust and drought never left her mind. The possibility of losing everything you worked for was awful. The Depression was now a reality as never before.

She never talked about it. But she feared it.

Would the Black Blizzards come to Rock Rapids, too?

Could Papa lose everything he worked so hard for?

Would the Depression ever end?

Chapter 9. September 1935

First Day of First Grade: A Song to Sing

"Katherine, Girl, will you hold still?"

"But, Mama, it hurts when you comb my hair so fast!"

"Well, you must not be late to your first day of school, must you?"

"Oh, but Mama, tell me again about school, please."

"Ach, Katherine, I have told you everything I know."

"Tell me . . . how long is the walk?"

"You were there with Willy at the end of last school year, remember?"

"Yes, I remember! The school is not very far away, is it?"

"No, Child. A section of land is a square mile. There is a school on nearly every section. That way children do not have far to walk and fathers don't have to drive them every day. You and Willy can easily walk to school."

"But you will take us to school in bad weather, right?"

"Of course. Papa would never let you to walk in heavy snow."

"Mama," Katherine's eyes were softly glowing, "tell me again what the school building looks like. Is it built of wood?"

"It has what is called a Wainscoting siding. It is a light beige color, almost white. It has one large room as a classroom, plus a wide porch entry for your coats and lunch pail."

"And, Mama . . ."

"That's enough, Katherine. I am finished with your hair. It is time to go. Let me look you over to see that everything looks right."

*   *   *

Five-year-old Katherine, ready for her first day at school, stood very still as her mother looked her over. Her hair, now combed neatly, was quite short and nearly straight. She was wearing one of the three little dresses which her mother had ordered from the *Sears, Roebuck & Co.* catalogue; she had also worn this dress last month on the trip to North Dakota.

The dress was made of an attractive plaid material, with tucks at the waist, hanging neatly to just below Katherine's knees. A belt at the waist was of the same plaid material. The dress had a white collar of which Katherine was quite proud. In her hair was a red ribbon attached to a rubber band.

Katherine's shoes were size 5, larger than she needed. They were sturdy black leather with little buttons up the front, sure to last until she outgrew them.

Susie gave a twist to straighten the dress, then nodded, satisfied.

"Time to go, Katherine," said Mama soberly.

Katherine reached eagerly for the small metal pail her mother handed her. The pail had been a syrup pail, emptied and cleaned so that it shone for Katherine's use. It was an aluminum color—very pretty, Katherine thought. And it had just enough room for Katherine's lunch.

"Oh, Mama," she chattered. "I do so like this lunch pail. But I won't look inside it until it's time for lunch. I want to be surprised."

*   *   *

Willie was patiently standing ready, also wearing his brand new first day clothing. He wore a new pair of farm coveralls from *Sears, Roebuck & Co.*

"You look nice, Willie!" Katherine told him. She was surprised when his face turned red.

Wilbur and Susie thought education was important enough to spend some of their meager money to buy good clothes for school. But Willie and Katherine must take very good care of these clothes so they would last as long as possible.

"Here, Willie, can you carry all the books?" Mama asked.

Willie looked proud of such an assignment. He was already eight years old, sturdy and tall for his age. Katherine, always a bit short for her age, thought Willie was very handsome. She was glad he was her brother.

Mama handed Willie two bundles of books, tied with two strings to separate them. The one held Willie's books and the other held Katherine's books. In each bundle were the required textbooks for school, which the parents bought ahead of time. Katherine's parents had gone early to the courthouse to buy their books at a discounted, used price.

Although the books had the names of former owners neatly printed inside the front cover, they had been well cared for with no writing on the lesson pages. All owners knew they could not resell the books if they were not taken care of.

Katherine had already studied the covers of the books. One book was for reading. Mama said it taught "phonics," an easy way to learn to read. Katherine had practiced out loud saying the alphabet to be ready for phonics.

Another book was for writing. With it went a tablet of writing paper to practice writing the alphabet letters.

A third book was for arithmetic. Katherine could already count to one hundred and hoped she would do well in that subject, too.

But the fourth book was the book of which Katherine was most proud. It was her first music book . . . which she saved all her life. It had a red cover and had many little songs which would be used in school. Katherine knew one of the songs, for Papa had often sung it: *Old McDonald had a Farm.*

"Goodbye now, Children." Mama smiled at both of them as she held open the door. Katherine held tightly to Willie's free hand as they crossed the freshly mowed lawn and walked down the gravel driveway to the country lane.

Before they reached the trees edging their acreage, she looked back once at Mama. Mama still stood in the open doorway of the house, waving with one hand while the other hand held the edge of her apron to her eyes. When Katherine stopped to watch her, she stepped back into the house, closing the door.

* * *

Willie and Katherine tried hard not to scuffle in the dirt because they wanted their shoes to last. But it was hard not to scuffle just a little.

Before long they saw other children walking down the lane, too. All school-aged children from the section went to this little country school.

There were six families in this square-mile section.

Altogether the six families had fifteen children in school. The Aaders had only one girl in the family. The Burrights had two boys and one girl. The John Folkens' family had two boys in school, Arent and Carl; a younger boy, Peter, was Dorothy's age. The Wulfsen family had two boys.

The Smidstra family was the largest, with five children in school: two older boys, two older girls and a girl named Jessie, a year older than Katherine. While Katherine was just starting first grade, Jessie would be in second grade this year. Katherine knew what she looked like from church.

"I hope we become friends," she thought. "It will be awful not to have a friend in school."

* * *

The school had a small sign in the front, made by one of the farmers who owned engraving tools. It read, *"Midland #3 School."*

Mama had told Katherine that there were several schools in the Midland County, one for each section in which there were enough children for a teacher. Each of the schools had one classroom and one teacher.

Katherine held very tightly to Willie's hand as they walked up to the small school. She hardly dared look at the other children. She was so tiny and timid! She didn't *really* know anyone.

* * *

Suddenly, a small, blonde-haired girl darted out from the group of Smidstra children. Katherine recognized her: Jessie Smidstra, the girl in second grade. Jessie ran up to Katherine and grabbed her hand.

"Katherine!" she exclaimed with a huge smile. "My mama told me you would start first grade. She told me I must help you. Is that okay?"

Katherine's eyes grew wide. Her smiled exploded on her face.

Was it okay? She would have a friend!

"Oh, yes!" she breathed softly. "Yes, please."

Willie was willing to let go of Katherine's hand but not her books. "I'll bring your books into school, okay?" Willie said. Katherine smiled at him and nodded happily.

While Willie walked ahead and joined two other boys, Jessie and Katherine walked together, holding hands. Inside the porch door, Jessie showed Katherine where to put her metal lunch pail on the shelf. She showed her where to hang her coat on the hooks when the weather got cooler.

Then Jessie showed Katherine where she would sit in the classroom. The first grade spot was right near the large, pot-bellied coal stove. That was so that in winter the littlest children would stay the warmest.

Katherine was the only student in the first grade. Some grades had more than one student but there were eight grades and only fifteen students, so some grades had no students at all, some grades had one student, some grades had two students, and one fortunate grade had three students.

Willie thought it was more fun if there were three students to a grade. Katherine thought it was just fine that she was alone for then she didn't have to worry that someone else would be smarter than she was.

As Jessie showed her where to sit, Willie came over to Katherine and gave her the four books which her parents had bought for her. Katherine touched them with pride. "It will be so much fun to read and write," she murmured to herself.

She watched how Jessie leaned down to slide her books into the open front of the desk and did the same with her own books. She took her two pencils and placed them carefully into the pencil slot, which was on top of the desk next to the inkwell. In first grade, she was too young, of course, to have any ink in the inkwell. Students learned to use ink in the fifth grade.

With just her two pencils, she was ready for school.

*　*　*

Well, almost ready, that is. She noticed students holding their new pencils and forming a line behind the pencil sharpener.

The school was proud of this new addition. The sharpener was a shiny silver color with gold embossing. It had a crank, a handle that you turned to make a sharpener inside it sharpen the pencil . . . and it would catch all of the shavings from the pencils. After awhile there were too many shavings and Katherine watched as Susie Smidstra emptied the shavings into a green metal garbage can.

Susie was the oldest student on Katherine's first day. The two older Smidstra boys would not be starting school until harvest was finished.

"Katherine, would you like to sharpen your pencils?" asked Jessie as she finished sharpening her own. Katherine nodded shyly as she retrieved the two pencils from her pencil slot. Jessie showed her how to hold a pencil through the hole in the sharpener while she turned the crank with her other hand. Katherine was pleased to see the shavings fall off her pencil and then pull out a nice, sharp point. It was fun to do.

*   *   *

Still sharpening her pencil, Katherine realized that the classroom had become quiet and the teacher was standing in front of the classroom waiting. Blushing, she hurried to her seat. But the teacher's smile was kind.

"Welcome to a new school year," said the teacher. "My name is Mavis Sands. You will call me Miss Sands. I will write my name on the board. Here it is: *M-i-s-s S-a-n-d-s*."

Miss Sands had long, light brown hair. She pulled it back into some kind of twist. Katherine wondered how she managed that twist. It looked really nice.

Some teachers taught school after just finishing high school but Miss Sands had two years of college, with teacher training. Katherine's parents had told Willy and her that she was a good teacher, kind and competent.

To begin the school day, they said the Pledge of Allegiance.

With the children following her example, Miss Sands stood erect, faced the American flag, placed her right hand over her left heart, and recited:

"I pledge allegiance to the flag
Of the United States of America
And to the Republic for which it stands:
One nation . . . indivisible,
With liberty and justice for all."

Willie had told Katherine about the Pledge of Allegiance and had even said it to her a few times, but she did not have it memorized yet. Still, it made her tingle to say it so solemnly with all the other students and the teacher.

Next, Miss Sands visited for awhile. She made sure everyone knew everyone else. Katherine tried to remember every name.

Miss Sands asked each student what had been special about the summer vacation. Willie told about the family trip to North Dakota last month. When it was Katherine's turn, Katherine slowly pulled out her red music book.

One boy snickered; everyone had a music book.

But Miss Sands understood.

"Do you like music, Katherine?" she asked kindly.

When Katherine shyly nodded, the teacher continued, "We will sing from the little red book before we go home today. Do you know any of the songs?"

Katherine whispered, "Yes. My papa sings one of the songs."

That was what made the first day of school special. A special second-grade girl who became Katherine's friend. A special teacher who understood Katherine's love of music. The red music book in her desk. And finally, at the end of the day, being able to sing from that red book.

Because, all her life, music was special for Katherine.

> "The tender love a father has for all his children dear,
> Such love the Lord bestows on them who worship
> him in fear."

Chapter 10. November, 1935, Part 1

"I love that baby so much . . ."

Five-year-old Katherine was second Mama to Baby Dorothy.

Mama was always so busy! When Mama was washing dishes or baking bread, she would tell Katherine to sing to the baby . . . or to rock the crib a bit. Sometimes Katherine would lie on her stomach next to the baby, on blankets in the small dining room next to the kitchen, and softly hum to Dorothy.

"I love that baby, Mama," Katherine once confided to Susie. "I just love her to pieces. I don't ever want her to cry."

That made Mama happy. Katherine knew because later she heard Mama repeat the comments to Papa.

*   *   *

At suppertime, Papa watched Katherine mothering Dorothy while Susie put food on the table. He had a bemused smile . . . which irritated Katherine.

"Why are you laughing at me, Papa?" she demanded.

"No, no, Little Princess, I'm not laughing at you," Papa teased her. "I'm just remembering another incident."

"What are you remembering?" asked Katherine.

She was always eager for stories. Papa told lots of them.

Papa responded, "I'm remembering when Gerrit was born. You were still just a toddler yourself at that time. You were born in June and he was born in May not even three years later. So you weren't quite three years old.

"But you were mighty bright for a little two-year-old! You could talk a mile a minute when you wanted to."

"Papa!" protested Katherine. "I don't talk too much!"

"You talked a lot, Little One. How else would you learn to think? Talking isn't bad, is it? But, you were usually quiet around strangers. I guess you didn't have enough practice in meeting other people."

Papa paused a moment to collect his thoughts.

"Well, back to Gerrit. After he was born, we had a lot of people around for awhile. There was the doctor. And his nurse. And a neighbor lady who helped Mama a few days. And a Kracht girl we hired to stay and help Mama for a few weeks. Right then, we had all kinds of people for you to get used to.

"One of the people who stopped in after Gerrit's birth was our minister, Rev. John De Jong. He stopped in just for a normal pastoral visit. He read the Bible to us, prayed with us, and shared in our joy over a new baby's birth.

"As he arrived, with people busy all over the house, he was met at the door by Willie and you. He first greeted Willie and then turned to talk to you."

"The minister talked to me all by myself?" exclaimed Katherine, somewhat awed. She never dared talk to ministers.

"Yes, he did. He knelt down next to you, because you were so little . . . and cute, my dear, so cute. He said to you, 'I hear you have a new baby in the house. Do you know his name?'"

Papa grinned again, obviously amused by the memory.

"You know what you answered the minister?"

Katherine shrugged. How was she to remember?

"You said, 'I think his name is . . . Kroontje!'"

Papa then roared with laughter, making the family laugh with him. "You were such an adorable tike, Katherine! So tiny but already using our surname.

"The minister never forgot that. We joke about it every time someone has a new baby. 'What is his name?' 'Oh, I think it must be . . . Kroontje.'"

* * *

Katherine had just started to school in September of 1935 when Mama found a used crib advertised. It was a sturdy metal crib, metal like a galvanized tub. The price was affordable so Mama bought it.

"A real baby mattress," Katherine oohed when she saw it. "Now Dorothy won't have to sleep on a corn husk mattress, will she, Mama?"

Mama smiled.

"Are you happy for her?" she asked kindly.

"Oh yes, Mama, of course I'm happy for her. The corn husk mattress makes me itch sometimes. The feed sack covering is stiff. I'm glad Dorothy won't itch."

"We'll have to change the husks in yours soon," said Mama thoughtfully. "I've been too busy before but the corn is already harvested and the husks are all in piles. I'll do that soon."

* * *

A few days later, Katherine came home from school to a real surprise. She went up the stairs to her room to change from her school dress to her chores' clothes. As she opened the door, she saw the metal crib against the window wall.

"Oh!" she whispered, careful not to wake the baby, "Dorothy is in my room now!"

The half-attic bedroom was so small, she couldn't have imagined that the metal crib would fit. Obviously, it had taken Papa and Mama some time to figure out how to manage it.

Everything was all squashed into the room: the corn husk bed along one sloping roof wall, the dresser a foot away from it on the inside wall, and Dorothy's crib along the outside wall.

In the corner near the crib, Mama had nailed a rod to hang their clothes. She had made a curtain of feed sacks to hang in front of the clothes. It was a make-shift closet.

Katherine had to walk sideways to get between the bed and crib. She peeked into the crib and saw Dorothy, all curled up in her cute pink kimono. For a long minute, she studied the precious tike. Slowly, she reached to touch her . . .

But then, the baby moved. Just a little, not waking up. But enough so that Katherine quickly stepped away. She didn't want to awaken her. Mama needed help with chores first.

*   *   *

Katherine was never told why Dorothy had been moved upstairs. But she figured it out later, much later. Mama was expecting another baby in the spring. So Dorothy must learn to sleep upstairs.

At bedtime, Katherine found that she had a new covering on her corn husk mattress. Mama had also been busy sewing.

To make the bed fresh, Mama had used new feed sacks with a new pattern. She sewed them together like a giant pillowcase and put fresh corn husks inside them. Then she sewed shut the open edge to make an enclosed mattress. It was almost as if Katherine had a new bed. Everything was fresh . . . even if it was still crinkly.

Katherine ran back downstairs.

"Mama!" she exclaimed with pleasure. "When did you go to town for new feed sacks?"

"Ach, Katherine, your father went to town for feed two or three times in the past months. I saved the feed sacks.

"Do you like the new patterns?"

"Oh yes, Mama! Thank you so much!" Katherine ran to Mama and gave her a hug. Mama's tired eyes shone as she hugged her back.

The mattress was still a corn husk mattress. It was still stiff and a bit scratchy. But Katherine felt loved as she crawled into it to sleep. Mama had done a lot of work for her.

Katherine's mattress was fresh.

And now Katherine had a roommate.

She didn't mind. She loved having a companion sister.

A sister was even better than a friend at school!

All their lives, these sisters would be best friends.

*   *   *

It was the Saturday before Thanksgiving.

Trees, which had been golden and red with autumn colors, were now bare of leaves. Only a single leaf hung here and there.

Threshing season was over. Hay, no longer green, was now in the barn loft or else stacked and covered with tarp behind the barn near the horse pasture.

The garden was now bare. Everything in it was canned. Except for potatoes. They had been piled in the cellar.

Apples had been picked from the trees. Winter apples, wrapped in newspaper, were stored in the cellar. Some apples had been canned for making pies. The rest had been canned as chunky applesauce.

The majority of the large birds had migrated south. Geese had flown overhead, honking their powerful cries as they flew in constantly changing V-formations.

Smaller birds were still stirring in the trees and bushes. In the winter, Mama Susie would scatter grain to feed them.

Large turkeys wandered in the pasture. One was fattening itself for Thanksgiving. The turkeys were a nuisance because they didn't stay in the pasture but wandered wherever they wished, sometimes even to the neighbors.

Katherine, babysitting Dorothy while Mama was busy, explained all these things to her. She wanted her sister to know.

*   *   *

The weather that November week was warm and balmy. Papa called it an Indian summer. Mama was happy because it gave her a few days to clean windows. She liked the windows cleaned inside and outside.

Cleaning windows kept Papa busy, too. He had to take out the summer screens, bring the winter storm windows from the barn for Mama to clean, and put the clean storm windows back into the window frames.

Window cleaning was hard work.

*   *   *

In between helping Mama, Papa was busy with another winter preparation. It was called "banking" the house. Banking was important because the house was old and drafty. Without banking, there was no way to keep the tiny farm house warm.

Willie helped Papa bank the house. Papa would place a strip of tar paper along the house. Willie would hold it in place while Papa would hold a plaster lat across the top and nail it in place. This would stop the winds from blowing into the house. Sometimes Papa would call Katherine to leave Dorothy and help also for a few minutes.

Around the tar paper banking, Papa placed straw bales. Everyone helped by dragging the bales to the house. Papa stacked them almost to the height of the windows. The straw bales plus the tar paper would insulate the house.

*   *   *

While Papa and Mama cleaned windows and banked the house, Katherine took care of Dorothy. The weather was so nice, she had Dorothy outside.

Katherine pushed Dorothy on the swing.

The swing was really an old tire. Papa had cut the tire in half. He had punched out holes in each end. Through the holes he had worked a strong rope, knotting the rope securely. He had used the rope to hang the half tire to a large branch of the huge old oak tree near the house. This tire was their "swing".

Dorothy loved the swing. Katherine had to be careful that Dorothy was sitting securely but then, with one hand holding her, she would gently shove the swing. The baby would squeal with delight . . . as long as Katherine didn't shove too fast.

"Isn't it beautiful out here?" Katherine murmured.

Baby Dorothy didn't answer in words. She just chortled.

"Wouldn't you like to live in a tree house?" Katherine continued to muse.

Dorothy squealed. She kicked her legs happily.

"If we lived in a tree house, we could pretend we were birds," Katherine continued her playful thoughts. "We could take food up in the tree, store it for winter just like the birds. And then we could let the winds howl . . ."

*   *   *

By the time the windows were all washed, the wind was coming up. Katherine was getting chilled. She held Dorothy to protect her from the chilly wind. She covered her own ears and then Dorothy's ears to warm them up.

Mama Susie saw their cold.

"Children, get inside the house!" she called to them. Glad that the storm windows were all in place, she was walking jauntily towards the house.

"Get a jacket on Dorothy, you hear, Katherine?" Mama chided. "You are cold, too, Girl. I don't want you both sick."

*   *   *

Ashamed that she had let Dorothy get cold, Katherine scurried to find a small coat which had been hers four years earlier. Because Katherine kept growing, Mama sewed a coat for her each year. Old jackets became Dorothy's.

Susie quickly brought Dorothy upstairs for a nap. Since the attic room was chilly, she kept the jacket on her besides covering her with a warm blanket. Katherine went outside to do the chicken chores while Susie got supper started.

Neither of them guessed how the next few hours would change the rest of November and December.

> "For indeed (she) was sick nigh unto death: but
> God had mercy on (her); and not on (her) only,
> but on me also . . ."

Dorothy

Chapter 11. November 1935 (continued)

Whooping Cough!

"Haw . . . aw . . . awk!"

Until that noise, it was a normal ending to a normal day. Chores were finished. Everyone was entering the house for supper. Papa and Willie were washing their hands. Mama was putting food onto the table. Katherine was setting the table with forks and knives.

Suddenly that awful sound came from upstairs. It sounded like a hoarse bark. Mama gave a gasp and nearly dropped the pan she was holding. Papa, entering the room from the porch, gave a quick glance at Mama and headed for the stairs. Katherine had never seen him move faster.

Three minutes later, Papa was back downstairs holding a sleepy Dorothy. She was rubbing her eyes, which seemed watery. Papa held a large handkerchief, wiping her runny nose.

What was the expression Papa had often chuckled about? "Parents who love their snot-nosed children . . ." Children often had runny noses.

Mama stepped over to Papa and placed her hand on Dorothy's forehead. Mama frowned. Dorothy did look a little flushed.

"The Sioux City Paper just had an article, Wilbur," said Mama with concern. "It said that there are several new cases of whooping cough in the state. It gave signs we should watch for. A runny nose and fever can be the start of whooping cough."

"Oh, Mama," countered Papa, "our children are always getting runny noses and slight fevers. That's part of being a child. Don't worry so easily."

"It's hard not to worry," Mama responded. "You know how many American children die of whooping cough? Five to ten thousand children each year! There have been years when 25,000 children died. It's a real killer!"

"Yes, but the girls just got chilled outside. Whooping cough comes from a bad bacteria. Were the children exposed to anyone else with whooping cough?"

"Not that I know of," Susie replied, looking somewhat relieved. "You are probably right. It's just a mild cold.

"But it's hard not to worry. The paper said that whooping cough is most severe in babies. Dorothy is only a year and five months old."

The family sat down to pray and eat.

Katherine kept watching Dorothy. If Dorothy got whooping cough, would it be her fault? Because she had let her get chilled outside?

*   *   *

Dorothy often had a runny nose. That wasn't unusual.

This time, though, she had a runny nose already for two weeks. Added to the runny nose were watery eyes, a red nose, and sneezing. And now she had that strange barking cough.

Mama had Watkins cough syrup in the house. She gave a large spoonful to Dorothy. Dorothy didn't seem to mind. She thought it was some new food.

After supper, Mama washed dishes and Katherine dried them. Dorothy sat on Papa's lap while he read the paper. Willie had some homework from school and was studying in the dining room by a kerosene lamp.

Dorothy occasionally coughed. Every time, Mama glanced at Papa. Papa usually ignored her but a few times he gave a slight nod.

Papa was reading the article about whooping cough, too.

He wanted to be prepared in case he was wrong.

How could they know if this was just a cold . . . or the bad thing? A normal cold . . . or whooping cough? Pertussis, the paper said. The killer cough. It was hard not to worry.

* * *

Everyone was in bed. It was the middle of the night. Katherine had been sleeping for a few hours. Suddenly she heard voices . . . right in her bedroom.

Papa and Mama were bending over the crib. Papa was holding the lantern and they both were watching Dorothy.

Katherine had been sleeping soundly. She hadn't heard Dorothy coughing again. But now she heard it. Dorothy's cough was much worse than at suppertime. It sounded very much like a hoarse bark. Getting worse each hour.

Katherine heard Papa's whisper.

"Yes, Susie, it is worse. We will get the doctor in the morning."

And she heard Mama's response.

"Is it safe to leave her up here?"

Papa answered, "Through these old walls, Susie, we can hear her just as easily downstairs. Her crib is up here and she can sleep better. Leave her here."

They didn't know that Katherine was awake now and heard them. They went back downstairs and to bed.

While they may have had trouble sleeping downstairs, Katherine was now fully awake and couldn't sleep upstairs. Every time Dorothy coughed the rest of the night, she heard.

It was a good thing it was Saturday with no school.

* * *

The coughing was bad enough.

Often the coughing lasted so long that finally Dorothy would expectorate. Mama said this was not bad; it was getting all the germs out. But Katherine felt so very sorry for Dorothy.

Day after day was the same. Katherine went to school but her mind stayed home. Would Dorothy be worse when she got home?

∗   ∗   ∗

Dr. Corcran came to their house to see Dorothy. He confirmed that she had Whooping Cough. The medical term was pertussis. There wasn't a lot that could be done for pertussis. In those years before antibiotics were discovered, the large majority of infants would die from it. They couldn't control their coughing. Infants would gag and choke on mucous in their throats.

Katherine loved Dr. Corcran. He always brought a treat when he came to the house. This time he gave them each an orange. Mama could never afford oranges so that was special.

∗   ∗   ∗

The family did *not* practice isolation with Dorothy.

The whole family was involved in caring for her. Papa and Mama set up an oxygen tent because she needed moisture. Everyone listened all the time for her coughing spells. If she began coughing, everyone would run to sit her up. The big danger was in lying down—then she couldn't breathe.

The hoarse "ha-aw-aw-awk!" had changed to a long "whoo-oo-oop!"

Katherine would never forget the sound of the whoop. First, Dorothy would suck in her breath in a long, long, drawn-in breath. Then, all at once the breath would go out in that horrible whoo-oop! It was that loud and forceful whoo-oop that had given whooping cough its name.

Papa and Mama moved Dorothy downstairs to sleep. They didn't want the other children to catch the sickness. But also, they wanted to be near her. Papa and Mama hardly got any sleep because they took turns all night long listening for her coughing and whooping.

And everyone prayed. Just knowing how often whooping cough led to death made everyone conscious of how close Dorothy might be to heaven. It made them feel a desperate need for God.

Katherine prayed every night before going to bed. On her knees, with her hands folded, she prayed earnestly. Over and over, she prayed one prayer. "Father in heaven, please take care of Dorothy. I'm sorry I let her get cold so she got sick. Please make her all better."

But her tears and prayers were never enough. She still felt guilty.

And she didn't dare tell anyone else what she was thinking. She had been taking care of Dorothy when she got chilled and the whooping cough began. If Dorothy died, would she be responsible?

*　　*　　*

Dorothy's whooping cough lasted nearly a month.

The house was a different place all during that month. Everyone kept everything quiet all the time. They were so afraid they wouldn't hear Dorothy when she needed them. They didn't dare to be busy with something that would make them not hear her. She could die so easily.

Katherine finally had to ask the question she was always thinking. "Mama, what if Dorothy dies? Couldn't God stop her from dying?"

Mama's eyes filled with tears. Although she was busy making supper, she held out her arms and hugged Katherine.

"Oh, Child, are you so afraid of her dying, too?"

"Mama, are you afraid of death?"

Mama Susie looked stunned at the question.

"No, Katherine, I'm not afraid of death. Jesus has died for our sins and I know God loves us. So I'm not afraid to die.

"And God has promised that He will be a God to us and our children. God loves Dorothy, too. She is His child even though she is only a baby and can't understand this yet.

"No, I'm not afraid of Dorothy dying, either. Not afraid.

"But, Katherine, I hate her suffering. And I love her so much I'm very selfish. I want to keep her here on earth. I'm afraid for myself, not for her."

Katherine had to ask the question she feared most.

"Mama, if Dorothy dies, will it be my fault for letting her get cold?" Tears pooled in her eyes as she asked the question.

"Your fault? Katherine, is that what you think? Child, if anything, it would be my fault for not noticing the wind. I am the mother and responsible. You are only a child.

"Besides," Mama added, "cold doesn't cause pertussis. Remember what Papa read? It's caused by bacteria. She must have been near someone else who was getting it."

Mama swallowed hard. She was usually quieter than Papa but she would say important things.

"Katherine, don't be afraid. You may cry, because we can't help that. God understands that we need to cry. But don't be afraid. God won't let anything happen unless it's the best thing.

"The best thing for us as well as for Dorothy."

*   *   *

The doctor said it was important to have healthy food. So Mama kept giving Dorothy little bits of soup broth and water. She never gave her too much at a time because she was afraid of expectoration.

Two nights before Christmas it became especially bad. The sounds of the coughing were *so awful*. Dorothy's head was *so hot* to the touch. Mama kept putting cool washcloths on her forehead. The whooping was dreadful. Except for that sound, the house was deadly silent. No one could think of anything else.

Papa finally couldn't stand the sound. He went outside for a walk. Katherine ran to her upstairs window to watch him and saw him leaning against a tree, his head bowed. His shoulders were shaking. She knew he was crying.

Then she saw him kneel next to the tree, his arms around the tree, his head still down. She knew that he was praying, too.

She wished she could go hug him . . . but it was too cold outside with only her nightgown on. Besides, she didn't dare.

Instead, she kneeled next to her cornhusk bed. Softly, she whispered out loud the words in her heart.

"Father in heaven, please be with Papa. He needs you real bad, God. Be with Mama. And with Baby Dorothy. Make her better. We love her so much. Please let us keep her yet."

And then, because she was still a child and because she was so very tired, she fell asleep, still kneeling next to her bed. She never knew when Papa came in and tucked her gently into bed.

*   *   *

That was the worst night. Mama called it the climax . . . the turning point. From then on, Dorothy rapidly grew better.

Katherine knew God had heard their tears and their prayers. She was so thankful that God had let Dorothy get better. So, so thankful!

Never would Katherine laugh about death. When other people made jokes about dying, Katherine remembered Dorothy's whooping cough. Death was not something to laugh and joke about. It was serious.

But life was wonderful. How wonderful to have Dorothy still alive! Katherine never complained about helping Mama take care of her.

She loved that baby sister so much!

Her recovery was the best Christmas present they could have.

> "Lay up for yourselves treasures in heaven . . .
> For where your treasure is, there will
> your heart be also."

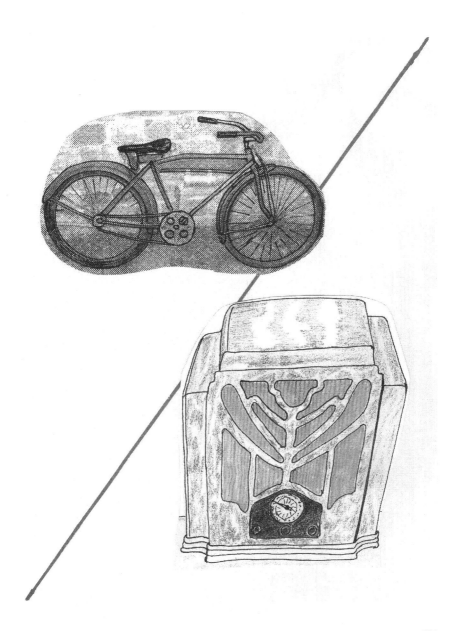

Chapter 12. September, 1937

Men and Boys Buy Toys

"Ahoy, Tony!" nine-year-old Willie called out to the young man who had just ridden a new bicycle onto the yard. "What are you riding? Why didn't you hitch a ride like usual?"

The young man, Tony, was a 15-year-old from Rock Rapids. He had recently become Wilbur's hired man. Wilbur had hired Tony because his young mother, prematurely widowed, could not feed and clothe her three children. Besides having lost her husband, she herself was not in good health.

Labor was inexpensive in the 1930s because no one could afford to pay much in the Depression years. Many teenagers worked for just room and board, maybe a bit of spending money for extra work. That already helped their parents out. In summer when there was field work, the pay was an added $1.00 per day.

Tony, however, lived at home. He had been catching a ride the eight miles from Rock Rapids until he arrived with his bicycle.

"Good mornin', Willie," the 15-year-old jauntily replied. "I've been savin' ever' penny your papa pays me for this bike. I finally had almost enough to buy it. How do you like it?"

"It's swell!" Willie replied. He walked around it, admiring the sleek blue color and the chrome handlebars with rubber ends. It would be so nice to have a bike like this for school. What did one cost? Was it worth dreaming about?

"Where did you get this bike?" he asked.

"Well, you know that new car lot in town?" answered Tony. "The one where your father bought his Model A Ford?"

Willie nodded. Did he know that car lot? Of course! He looked at that car lot every time they went to town.

"Well," continued Tony, "they also sell bicycles. I have stopped there several times, wondering if I could ever afford one. It would be nice to bicycle from Mom to here. Plus, then I could work more often instead of just when I found a ride."

Willie noticed a tear in Tony's eyes. He understood.

"Usually two or three bicycles are sitting there," continued Tony. "Some Schwinns. Some Columbias. Sometimes another brand.

"But I didn't want to buy one until I could pay for it outright. No charges for me, no sir! Besides, right now people won't let you buy things on credit."

"You haven't worked for Papa long enough to pay for a bike like this, have you?" asked Willie in surprise.

"No, definitely not," responded Tony. "I only started working two months ago. And half my earnings go to Mom."

"But then . . . ?" puzzled Willie. He scratched his head.

"But then, another young man ordered a bike," replied Tony. "The salesman said he paid half the money ahead of time, which is required. But he couldn't come up with the other half of the money. So he lost not only the bicycle but also his down payment on the bicycle.

"Well, I feel sorry for him. But his loss is my gain, I guess. He should have made sure he had all the money before he paid half of it, right?

"Anyway, I was checking out bicycles one day. The salesman came up to me and made me an offer. I could have this bike for just the remainder of the payment, what was still owed."

"What a deal!" exclaimed Willy.

"What a deal, indeed! I didn't have enough money, but I asked him to hold the bicycle while I checked it out. Your father said he could loan me the difference. So I paid it, owe your father something, but now own a bicycle.

"What do you think?"

Willie's eyes were wide with admiration.

"I wish I had been given that deal," he responded. He couldn't resist rubbing his hands over the shiny chrome again.

"If it were mine, I would be scared something would happen to it."

*   *   *

Just then Wilbur and four-year-old Gerrit came from the house together. It was still early, the predawn sun just peeking over the horizon. Morning chores had to be done before breakfast. Wilbur valued hard work. His children were taught at an early age to rise early for chores.

"Good mornin', Tony!" Wilbur called out cheerfully. "I see you arrived nice and early. Good for you!

"And what's this? Got your new vehicle?" Wilbur admired the bicycle. Its indigo color glistened in the rising sun.

Tony's eyes shone with his boss' admiration.

"Fine bicycle, Tony. A Schwinn, standard of the industry. I see you even have the balloon tires which were introduced only three years ago. It's a bike worth working for, indeed.

"Young Man, we had better get to work so this bicycle gets paid for, you think?" he nodded. "All right, Boys. Let's get at 'er!"

"Uh, Boss, do you think I could keep this bicycle inside the barn somewhere?" asked Tony anxiously. He did not want anything to happen to his bicycle before it was even paid for!

"Why, of course," replied Wilbur at once. "Put it in the corner, okay?"

Tony agreed. He was glad he worked for Wilbur.

As the screen porch door slammed shut again with Katherine coming out to do her share of the chores, Tony and the boys were clearing a spot in the barn for the new bike.

*   *   *

At supper one day, following a trip to town, Wilbur laughingly repeated a comment by a neighboring farmer.

"Question: How does a boy differ from a man?

"Answer: A boy buys little toys. A man buys big toys."

Grinning, Wilbur confirmed: "It's true, isn't it? Tony bought a Schwinn. I bought a Model A Ford. Katherine buys a red music book. And I buy . . ."

Well, the answer is the rest of this chapter . . .

*   *   *

Up until the 1930s, the Kroontjes got all of their news through the newspapers. Even newspapers were considered a luxury and so neighbors would sometimes buy and share a daily newspaper. Once a week, they would meet in town to learn all the news and then the newspaper would be passed on to someone else. All of them were hungry for news.

So the development of the radio was popular news. Newspapers reported what radios said. Every so often, one neighbor . . . and then another neighbor . . . would save up money to buy a radio. Everyone marveled at the invention.

Radios had actually begun broadcasting just about the time the Kroontjes got married. Each year after 1925, more and more broadcasts were aired. By the 1930s, even though the Depression was on and finances were tough, more and more news-hungry people were squeezing out the finances for radios. People were hungry for news, any news.

People were also hungry for fun. Other than local picnics, parades and fairs, they had little entertainment. Radios gave them politics and news and sports *and entertainment.*

And all this, mind you, for a relatively inexpensive price. Some financial genius had figured out a way to keep radios cheap: let advertisements pay for broadcasting! Few people minded the advertisements; it was good also to know what new things could be purchased. How nice of business people to pay for their listening so they could afford to buy a radio!

*   *   *

In the early years of their marriage, Wilbur and Susie never considered buying a radio. Radios were, they thought, a luxury. Radios didn't always work. News on them was sporadic.

But radios improved. Politics were important, and they began hearing more and more about President Roosevelt's Fireside Chats. Roosevelt was working hard to stem the Depression. A few times, they went to town specially so they could sit and listen to these chats. It was the Fireside Chats that convinced Wilbur. He must have a radio!

Besides that, radios caught on so quickly that before long local news were also being broadcast. News became very important. Farmers were all tuning in to weather broadcasts.

Not that weathermen were trusted.

"Hey, you know what that weather guy said last week?" one farmer chortled as he shared with the other farmers listening eagerly around the hardware store heater. "He said it was going to freeze last Thursday night! All you fellas remember, don't you? What happened on Thursday night?"

A neighbor scratched his beard as he recalled, "I distinctly recollect that last Thursday it warmed up and we had an Indian summer come Friday. Yes, sir, an Indian summer. 80 degrees, it was. Does that weatherman know anything?"

But, even though weathermen were often wrong, the farmers listened. They just might know something of importance. They just might be right next time.

And so Wilbur, in the post-election year of 1937, invested in his first radio. Not only could it maybe tell him the weather when it was important, but it could give him Roosevelt's Fireside Chats.

*   *   *

Susie bought a little table for the radio. She was in the store and heard one advertised over the store radio. It was right in town and she was first to arrive to offer to buy it. That made the radio worth its cost, right there. It paid for itself!

If they had to, they could even drop their subscription to the Sioux City Paper. For a radio, they only needed to buy batteries. To operate, the radio needed a 6 volt battery, about the size of a car battery. The radio fit on the front of the sturdy little table Susie bought. The battery fit right behind it.

"Where is the best place to keep the radio, Wilbur?" asked Susie. She thought it best to keep such an important item in the dining room, in a corner out of the way of harm.

"I think in the kitchen," Wilbur responded, "for two reasons. First, it will be easier to string the wire through the kitchen window to the barn. That will mean good reception for us. Second, we can listen as a family while we are relaxing. You can even listen as you work. Won't it make your work more fun if you can listen to a radio at the same time?"

Susie was delighted. It was true. While she baked her bread, she could listen to *Your Neighbor Lady*, a program for women with recipes and chatty housewifery. As she did dishes, she could tune in to *Ma Perkins* or to *Judy and Jane*. She could entertain the family at supper by retelling the latest news.

The children were mesmerized by the radio. They watched as Wilbur pored over its instructions.

The radio needed a wire to catch the signals which came through the air. Wilbur strung a wire from the kitchen to the barn. He tied it first to a screw on the radio, then stapled it onto the side of the house above the kitchen window, and then onto the side of the barn. He strung it high up so nothing would hit it.

*   *   *

Papa's favorite program, other than weather and news, was the *Lone Ranger* program. He knew it was fiction but he and other farmers liked to follow the Lone Ranger's exploits.

Katherine loved the radio, too. From her parents, she learned to listen carefully to important programs, such as political news or weather.

But her favorite programs were of two other kinds.

She enjoyed children's stories, especially. The only radio channel they could always get was WNAX from Yankton, South Dakota. Sometimes it carried Christian children's programs created by WMBI in Chicago.

Katherine's other favorite programs were music programs. The haunting tunes became her tunes. As she was doing chores outside, or cleaning upstairs, she was singing or humming, songs she learned on the radio.

> *"When He cometh, when He cometh, to make up His jewels,*
> *Precious jewels, precious jewels, His loved and His own . . .*
> *Like the stars of the morning, His bright crown adorning,*
> *They shall shine in their beauty, bright gems for His crown."*

How she enjoyed that radio! It brought outside life into her life. And it brought music. Wonderful, wonderful music.

> *"Whatsoever the Lord pleased, that did He . . .*
> *He maketh lightnings for the rain . . ."*

Chapter 13. July, 1937

Lightning Strikes

Wilbur and Tony rubbed down the sweating horses, which had been pulling the cultivator through the fields all day. Willie was also in the barn, giving the horses water and feed.

Wilbur always took thorough care of his horses. High quality feed. Good housing. The best care. This was obvious in the shine of their coats, in their sturdy strength, and in their cooperation with him.

It was late Friday afternoon. They had been cultivating corn all week.

"A good day's work out there!" Wilbur enthused as he rubbed his side of the horse. "One more day like this and the corn will be all cultivated. Makes a man feel good, aye?"

"Yes, sir," replied Tony with enthusiasm. He appreciated it that Wilbur talked with him man-to-man, not like a little kid. "One more day and we should be finished with the cultivating, Mr. Kroontje."

Wilbur glanced up through the open door at the sky. He frowned as he felt a rise in the wind and saw darkening clouds gathering overhead.

"We'd better hurry to get the chores done," he said. "You are already planning to stay with us overnight, Tony, and that is good. Because it sure looks like bad weather is coming. I hope it isn't so bad it damages the crops."

Katherine and Gerrit had just come outside as well. With the family growing in number, chores had also increased.

For now, Susie wasn't doing any chores. Two years earlier she had a miscarriage. She was never as strong again. That was one reason Wilbur had gotten a hired man, so Susie could spend less time outside and could manage her indoor work. With four children, she had plenty of work to keep her busy.

*   *   *

The wind picked up in speed. Wilbur listened to the growing wind with concern. Finally, he set aside his milk pail.

"Tony and Willie," he queried, "can you two handle the milking alone? I want to go check the weather station—hear what is blowing in."

"Yes, sir!" Tony and Willie answered together. They were proud that Wilbur trusted them to work alone. And they also wanted to know the forecast.

Wilbur's radio was still kept in the kitchen of the house. Glancing overhead as he left the barn, Wilbur could see the wire strung across the yard.

Susie was surprised to see Wilbur enter the kitchen so early. She had just taken bread from the oven and was beginning preparations for supper. But as Wilbur headed for the radio, she studied the darkening sky, felt the house vibrate with the wind, and understood. She, too, wanted the forecast.

The radio was still next to the window on the small, sturdy table Susie had bought. The table held both the radio and the 6-volt, car-sized battery which gave the radio its energy.

In bad weather, signals were hard to pick up.

Wilbur turned on the radio, already loud with static. It was hard to hear. Wilbur turned the knob between stations until he was able to pick up WNAX from Yankton. By pressing his ear close to the radio, he could make out words.

"It doesn't sound good, Susie," commented Wilbur, ear pressed to the radio. "There is a whale of bad weather pushing in from the southwest. It will be a real southwester. Wind, rain, possibly hail. Definitely thunder and lightning. We must make sure the livestock are all safe. I'll go back out to tell the boys."

*   *   *

Wilbur hadn't been inside the house more than fifteen minutes. The "boys" had worked hard and milking was nearly finished when he returned. Working together, they finished all the chores before the storm hit. When it arrived, they had already washed up and were sitting down to supper.

A small farmhouse is not an ideal place to be when a storm is howling outside. Every sound of the wind is exaggerated. This was a real storm and made so much noise it was hard to hear each other talk in the kitchen. If they hadn't wanted to eat supper first, they would have headed down into the cellar. It wasn't safe in the house.

Although Susie had prepared a good everyday meal, no one spent much time thinking about the food on the plates. All eyes kept roving to the swaying tree branches outside the windows. All ears kept listening to the thunder and the howling wind, hearing the tree branches bang against the house with the wind.

They were just ready to eat dessert pudding when an extra loud thunder sounded outside. Everyone jumped and turned towards the window. They had seen it at the same time as they heard it. A thick, jagged bolt of lightning streaked past the window and towards the barn. It made a loud c-r-a-c-k as it struck the barn door. Everyone heard the sound of splintering wood as the barn door cracked into pieces. What power lightning had!

It took only seconds for Papa Wilbur to stand and stride towards the porch door to look outside. "Boys!" he called back, "I am smelling sulfur. Let's get out there as fast as possible to take care of the animals. If that barn gets on fire, the lives of our cows and horses will be in jeopardy. Quickly!"

*   *   *

Katherine wanted to help, too, but knew she would be more trouble than help. She was too young to handle horses. As the men left the house, she stood with her nose pressed against the window, watching.

That's why she was first to see something surprising. It took her a few minutes to realize what she was seeing. She could only see when new lightning would flash.

"Mama," she called, "come look. What are those pieces of wood sticking out of the tree?"

Mama Susie, busy cleaning up two-year-old Dorothy, walked over with the washcloth still in her hand. She waited for another flash of lightning and then she, too, gasped.

"Oh, my! Those are splinters of wood! Katherine, those are pieces of the barn door you are seeing. When the lightning hit the barn, it must have splintered the door so badly that the wood flew in all directions. We will definitely need a new barn door!"

*   *   *

Papa, Tony and Willie were in the barn. Their job was to get the horses and cows out to safety. They could still smell the strong sulfur smell left when the lightning struck the door. The door was split right in half. The lightning had charred the door and it was smoldering. Papa was afraid it could burst into flames at any time.

The biggest danger was not the door itself but the hay in the overhead loft. The sulfur smell was also in the hay. If there was a smoldering fire underneath the hay, and if the hay ignited, it would be only minutes before the entire barn was in flames. That had Wilbur worried.

But something else made Wilbur angry. While he was rushing to get to the animals and save their lives, Tony was off in the corner trying to save his bicycle. That bicycle was his pride and joy; he did not want it destroyed by fire!

And so, before he would help with the horses, Tony's first thought was to save the bicycle. He quickly got it out and ran it across the yard to the garage which housed the Model A. Struggling against the wind, Tony managed to get the side door open and get his bicycle inside. Normally that would only have taken a minute. But, fighting the strong storm wind, it took Tony several minutes. Several *precious* minutes . . .

*   *   *

Meanwhile, Wilbur struggled with the horses. They were terrorized by the storm and were hard to manage. Papa needed two sets of hands to handle them. While Tony was getting his bicycle into the garage, Papa got very little done alone. It took two strong men to handle a high-strung horse.

Willie was too young to help very much. His job was to open and shut the stall doors and to get things that were needed.

When Tony finally was back in the barn, Papa was extremely angry. "What's more important," he yelled at Tony, "a bicycle or these horses? You're hired here to be helping!"

Tony was ashamed that he had only thought about his bicycle. "I . . . I'm sorry, Sir," he apologized, hanging his head. "I guess I wasn't thinking straight."

Now Tony tried as hard as he could to help. Together, Wilbur and he managed to get one horse at a time out of the barn and to the pasture behind the barn. Once the horses were safely out, they led the cows out. Although there was some danger of lightning outdoors, the rain wouldn't hurt them and they would be safe in case of fire.

*　　*　　*

Within one hour, the storm was over. Black clouds still swirled to the east, where the storm was now hitting. But the sky overhead was nearly clear.

The lightning strike had not, fortunately, led to a fire. Although the sulfur smell was still strong in the barn, the hay had never ignited. Only the barn door was ruined.

Now the cows and horses had to be gotten from the pasture and led back into the barn. It was not easy, because the animals were still nervous. Katherine, watching from the window, could see the horses rearing up in fear, could see how Papa tried to soothe them, how everyone had to work together to get them back into the barn.

At last everything was calm again. The cows were in their side of the barn, the horses in the other side.

The only thing different was the barn door. They had dragged it back into place but it was really useless now. Even a small shove could have made it collapse. Replacing that door would be the first thing on Papa's agenda tomorrow.

*　　*　　*

Since she had been in the house, Katherine hadn't seen Tony trying to save his bicycle rather than the horses. She heard about that later from Mama. Mama was slow to forgive Tony.

But Katherine did overhear Papa talking with Tony on the porch. Papa talked with him for about five minutes before they came back into the kitchen. By then they seemed to have everything straightened out between them. Tony looked shame-faced but Papa had his arm around his shoulders.

*　　*　　*

Mama had gotten out oil lamps and set them on the table. The storm had interrupted their meal. Now they would finish and have devotions.

Everything had become fairly calm outside. Only an occasional sweep of rain reminded them of the strong storm which had just occurred. Glancing out the window when distant lightning lighted the outdoors, Katherine could still see the wood splinters in the tree.

"Susie," Papa said while eating, "the next time there is a storm like this, we are using flashlights and taking the family into the cellar. Today was too dangerous up here."

Susie nodded. She agreed. Everyone else felt the same way.

With the pudding finished, Papa picked up the family Bible. Looking at Katherine, Papa asked, "Katherine, have you learned any Bible verses about storms?"

Katherine shook her head; she hadn't.

"How about the rest of you?" Papa asked.

Katherine was proud when Mama was able to respond, "Yes, *Psalm 135* is about storms. I read it just the other day."

So Papa read *Psalm 135* for their supper devotions. Katherine never forgot some of the things he read:

> *"Praise ye the LORD . . .*
> *"I know that the LORD is great . . .*
> *"Whatsoever the LORD pleased, that did He . . .*
> *"He causeth the vapours to ascend from ends of the earth;*
>   *he maketh lightnings for the rain;*
> *He bringeth the wind out of His treasuries . . ."*

God was great. He was in control when a storm came. Storms could never hurt anyone who loved Him . . . apart from God's will.

Apart from God's Fatherly love!

That gave Katherine comfort.

For that night, anyway, she was able to sleep without fear.

A Light Draft Binder Cutting Grain in a Deere Experimental Farm – page 137 of SOIL CULTURE
by J.E. McDougall & Son, early 1900s.

Chapter 14. July 1938 Part 1

Preparation for Threshing

It was the best of the best of times.

The children loved everything about oat threshing.

Oat threshing was a neighborhood affair. All the men gathered at one farm, then the next, and then the next. Each farmer took along a wagon and two horses. If a farm was small, its threshing might be finished in an afternoon. Wilbur's threshing took two days to finish. He raised lots of oats.

Excitement! Noise! Adventure! Big machines! Friendship! All rolled together in a bundle of euphoria! What more could any child want?

* * *

July was threshing time . . . time to harvest the oats.

Katherine didn't have to ask why Papa harvested oats. She had grown up with oats and knew all about them. She remembered kneeling with Papa in the field last spring while he examined an oat plant and told her about it.

The oat plant grew to about four feet high. It was a pretty, bushy plant. It was a dark green color until about a month before harvesting. Then it changed into a golden tan. The little husks became the same color as the oat inside. "There are red, brown and black oats in other places," Papa told Katherine. "Ours is the common oat. They say it is tan . . . but it gleams like gold in the sun. It is worth more than gold; you can't eat gold!"

Papa could explain things well. He was a good teacher.

Papa explained more.

"Oats are the most common of any grain, used around the world. Russia produces the most oats. The United States is second. All the Midwest states raise oats."

Willie knew some things from school.

"Teacher says there are two ways of growing oats," Willie interrupted. "In the southern states, oats are planted in the fall and harvested in the spring."

Papa's oats were planted as soon as the ground thawed in the spring. They would be ready to harvest by mid-summer.

"Does anyone raise oats to sell, Papa?" asked Katherine.

"Good question!" Papa praised Katherine. "People sell oats if they can't use them. They might have land but not livestock, like we do."

Papa didn't grow oats to sell. His oats were for the animals. The oat kernels, stored in the barn loft, were the main food for horses. The oat husk became straw for bedding.

Papa had most of his farm in oats. His other crops were soybeans, sorghum, corn and hay. All the crops were for the animals. Good oats made healthy livestock.

*   *   *

Mama Susie spent a whole week preparing for threshing. Oh, my! The food she had to prepare! She anticipated a whole crew of hungry men to feed each morning, noon and afternoon for two days.

Even on a depression food budget, farm women were expected to come up with competitive meals. Farm men would talk about the various meals whenever they got together. No woman wanted to be found lacking in culinary skills.

Mama had one thing in her favor from the start. She made the best homemade bread of anyone. She made unbeatable sandwiches to serve in the morning and afternoon along with other delicacies. Using the same bread dough, she made rolls to serve with her noon meal. There wasn't a farmer alive who didn't love her wonderful bread and rolls.

"What shall I put on the bread?" she worried.

Wilbur smiled reassuringly. "It doesn't matter, Susie," he responded. "We love your bread with anything on it."

"Well," Susie countered, "it can't just be jelly."

"*Your* rhubarb-mulberry jelly, Susie, is unbeatable!" Wilbur responded, licking his lips. "However, you could balance it with dried beef sandwiches. Or, think of all that good canned beef, canned chicken, and canned sausage in the cellar. Any of it would be great.

"And, of course . . ." with a twinkle in his eye . . . "we need a few cookies to go with it! We need energy, you know . . ."

Susie laughed, calmed by Wilbur's playfulness.

"Oh, go on with you!" she chuckled. "I guess sandwiches and cookies will work for the snacks, along with coffee and cold drinks. Now, what shall we have for the noon meal . . . ?"

*   *   *

Eight-year-old Katherine kept busy helping Mama. Mama wanted the house completely clean for "visitors". She also had to organize the eating. It was too hot to eat outside so she set up tables and benches in the cramped dining room. The men had to eat in shifts. Not all fit inside at once.

"Katherine, put a water pail under the oak tree outside," Mama instructed. "The men must wash up before dinner. Hang a mirror on the tree so they can see themselves. Also put a water basin and comb there."

"Will they want water to drink as they work?" asked Katherine. It was hot and she knew how thirsty heat made her.

"Yes, it will be the job of the boys to keep pumping water and ladling it into pitchers to bring the men," Mama answered. "They won't stop anymore than necessary, though. Once men start working, they want the work finished."

"Will I be able to watch them?" Katherine wondered. She wished she could be the one to bring the men their water!

"Oh yes, Katherine, you will help bring the morning and afternoon snacks," Mama replied. "The men take only short breaks, resting under a shady tree. The boys carry the drinks. You carry the sandwiches. Use the dishpan to carry them."

That satisfied Katherine. She didn't want to be out in that awful heat, anyway. But neither could she stay away.

*   *   *

Besides helping Mama, both Willie and Katherine were busy for a week ahead, helping Papa to get ready. They had to cut and bundle all the oats into shocks before threshing day could begin.

"Just imagine if you lived in the 1800s," Papa said to them. "Then a farmer would come out here with just a sharp sickle and cut all his oats by hand. His wife would follow him, making the bundles. Later they would go around the field to make the bundles into shocks. It would take weeks to do the job that we now can do in one or two days.

"I'm thankful that the binder was invented, aren't you?"

The binder was a fascinating machine. It had a set of sickles so it could cut several rows of oats at once.

As the oats were cut, they fell onto a 3' wide belt, which rotated as the horses walked. This belt moved the oat plants up the side of the binder machine onto a second belt.

The second belt—a wide canvas—moved the oat plants to an apparatus which tied the plants into bundles. Another mechanism dropped several bundles at a time onto the field. People called "shockers" would follow, setting the bundles into upright shocks to dry in the hot sun. The oats had to be in the air, the straw towards the bottom.

Papa sat on a seat. He held the reins to control the horses. He had to watch the entire binder machine, making sure everything went right. He also had to pull the lever to make the bundles drop when there were enough bundles tied. His job was very important.

Willie and Katherine were "shockers", setting the oat bundles upright. It didn't matter to the machine if they got behind. It would keep going. They could always come back tomorrow to finish.

Setting up oat bundles was difficult work for a small girl. Later Katherine would call it "child labor". She never forgot how heavy those bundles were.

*   *   *

By the time threshing day came, the shocks of oats were dry. They all hoped it wouldn't rain before threshing. Not only would rain delay threshing, but the oats would be poorer quality.

Mama was ready with the food. She had baked several pies. Papa put a block of ice in the galvanized pan in the cellar so the pies wouldn't spoil.

Papa had also spent a week helping other farmers to thresh. He took along one hay rack and two horses every day. Willie and Katherine did chores without him on those days.

Now it was their turn for threshing.

Katherine couldn't sleep for excitement. Everything for two weeks had been building to this point. Tomorrow was the big day, the most exciting day of the whole year.

> "The Lord giveth . . .
> Blessed be the name of the Lord!"

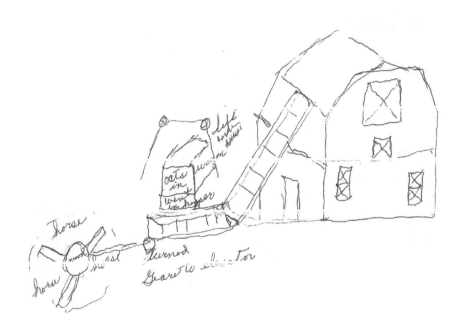

Chapter 15. July 1937 Part II

Threshing . . . and the Dorothy Scare

Long before the sun rose on threshing day, Willie and Katherine were outside with Papa getting chores done. They were so excited, they hardly slept the night before. Katherine had wiggled all night in anticipation.

The sun was scarcely up and the oats dry enough when neighboring farmers arrived with their hay racks—later called flatbeds. Each hay rack, pulled by two horses, headed for the fields.

Katherine heard the loud whistle of the approaching tractor and threshing machine. She could hear the whistle a mile away. The farmer who owned them was having fun.

Threshing machines were expensive. Several farmers might go together to buy one and then share it. Or else one farmer would buy a machine and other farmers would pay him for its use. Wilbur paid a farmer, who spent several weeks going around and threshing oats. The thresher was his sideline business.

The huge threshing machine, pulled by a huge tractor, drove to the large pasture behind the barn. The tractor was the power to make the threshing machine operate.

* * *

In the yard near the house, at the side of the barn, Papa's tall elevator was in place. The top of the elevator was over the open roof door to the barn loft, ready for oats to drop into the barn.

Everything was now ready. Threshing could begin.

*   *   *

Although farmers worked all day, they came in shifts. Some farmers liked to be on early shifts. If they started earlier, they could also quit earlier.

The job of the farmers was to get the shock bundles from the field. They used pitchforks. It was fun to watch them pitch oat bundles into wagons. A really good pitcher could pitch a whole shock into the wagon in one heave. It wasn't fussy how the shocks landed in the wagon; the thresher didn't care.

The farmers kept the thresher supplied with oat bundles. As soon as a loaded flatbed reached the yard, the farmer in the wagon dropped his oat bundles into the thresher chute. If everything was efficient, the thresher never had to wait.

The thresher's tractor turned a shaft attached to a pulley. This pulley pulled oat bundles up into the air where they were dropped into the heart of the threshing machine.

The first pulley also activated a second pulley which caused vibrations in the heart of the machine. The vibrations shook the oat plants so the oats fell off the straw. The oats shook through a screen onto a shaft out of the side of the machine. There oats fell from a spout into a regular farm wagon. When the wagon was full, it was pulled to the front yard so oats could be put into the barn.

The same vibrations shook the straw way up onto an elevator. The elevator went high up into the air, high enough so that the chaff straw would fall to a pile on the ground. The pile grew higher and higher as threshing continued.

That pile—a huge, huge pile—was used all year long. Papa used a pitchfork to get straw from the pile as bedding for the animals. The straw's use was to keep animals dry and warm.

All this threshing was powered by the tractor. Earlier, *horses* had been used. Some men used *steam engines* as the power. *Tractors* had been the next improvement. In the future, the entire system would be replaced by *combines*.

*　　*　　*

Katherine wanted to watch everything at once. How could she be in the field and yard at the same time? Her mind reviewed the entire process:

Step 1: BINDING: bind oat plants into bundles. Papa's job. Finished.
Step 2: SHOCKING: stand 6 bundles into shocks. "Her" job. Finished.
Step 3: TRANSPORTING: get shocks to the thresher. The farmers' job.
Step 4: THRESHING: thresh the oats, with a straw pile staying on the ground behind the barn and the oats going into the wagons. The thresher's job.
Step 5: ELEVATING: get the oats up into the front barn loft. Papa's job.

It was hard to choose which the most exciting step. They kind of all rolled together. But probably Step 5 was her favorite . . . because she loved watching the powerful horses.

*　　*　　*

While she was working in the house with Mama, Katherine often paused to watch Step 5. Step 5 occurred right in the yard, by the barn, about fifty yards from the house.

Farmers would haul wagons full of oats from the threshing machine to the yard. The wagons would back up to the elevator hopper. Over the wagon was a "lift", a neat concoction which used pulleys to lift the front of the wagon so the oats would slide to the back. The back of the wagon had a "gate", a door which could be lifted so that the oats would slide out onto the hopper. If the gate was lifted too high, too many oats would slide out.

A belt under the hopper and elevator lifted the oats up the elevator into the barn loft. Little shelves (or flaps) on the elevator held the oats, stopping them from sliding back down to the hopper. It was fun watching the oats go up, up and up, reach the top, then fall into the barn while the elevator shelves turned underneath and came back down on the underside.

Katherine knew that a wall separated the barn loft into two halves, half for oats and half for hay. In the side for oats, there was a trap door with a chute. When they needed oats, they could open this chute door and oats would slide down for them to feed the horses.

The trap door was a useful contraption—but it had dangers, too. Papa had warned of a young neighbor girl who got caught in the heavy trap door and was strangled before anyone could help her.

*   *   *

The best part of Step 5 was the way the elevator was powered.

Attached to the hopper was a shaft which had to be turned to make the elevator belt revolve. This shaft was powered by horses. Three horses would go around and around in the yard, pulling a mechanism in the center of the yard which made a shaft go around, which made the elevator belt go around. Horses were the power. They worked in two hour shifts, for two hours going around and around and around.

Pulling the elevator shaft was tiresome work for the horses. They had to pull and pull and pull, without stopping, very steadily. That was why every two hours they switched to pulling wagons from the fields.

Katherine loved to watch the powerful horses going around and around. As they walked, the dirt become soft where they walked. By the time they were finished, they had made soft dirt piles for the children to have fun.

*   *   *

It was getting towards evening on the first day of Papa's threshing. All day long, farmers had hauled bundles from the fields. All day long, farmers had fed bundles into the thresher. All day long, the thresher had been chugging and blowing straw into a pile. All day long, wagons had carried threshed oats to the elevator. All day long, three horses had gone round and round, churning up soft dirt as the elevator lifted the oats into the loft. The whole exciting process went on and on.

Mama was inside the house, preparing supper. Katherine had just brought the men their late afternoon snack of dried beef sandwiches and cookies plus fresh-squeezed lemonade. She sat for a few minutes under her cottonwood tree, listening to the chugging machine, watching the horses plod around and around. It was mesmerizing.

Katherine was tired from being up so early. Her eyes closed and her head began to nod. It had been a long day.

Suddenly she woke up to a shout from Mama. Mama was flying out of the house, shouting for all she was worth.

Looking where Mama was going, Katherine's heart nearly stopped.

Little Dorothy, still a toddler not even three years old, had headed for the horses. She saw the soft piles of dirt the horses were making and wanted to play in the dirt. Heedless of the chugging machine and the powerful horses in their circuit, she saw only the dirt. She toddled over to the dirt, sat down in it and began to sift the soft dirt through her fingers.

If the horses didn't stop, they would trample Dorothy to death!

Katherine jumped up also and began to run.

But suddenly, both Mama and Katherine stopped, amazed.

Prince, one of the brown horses doing the pulling, also saw little Dorothy. He stopped when he reached her, with one leg over her, protecting her. The other two horses kept pulling but Prince was strong enough to stop them.

The entire elevator had to stop because Prince had stopped. The farmer by the wagon shut the gate to the hopper to stop the oats from piling sky high.

Mama stood there, unashamedly weeping as she watched Prince. She threw her arms around him and hugged him. Then she bent and removed little Dorothy, scolding her, spanking her and hugging her all at one time.

While Mama took Dorothy back into the house, the three horses again began walking. The elevator again began rotating. And Katherine, now completely awake, ran into the house to help Mama and to protect her little sister.

She was surprised to find Mama just sitting in a chair. Mama never just sat, never! But she was shaking so badly, all she could do was hold little Dorothy.

Dorothy didn't even realize what a scare she had caused. She was trying to wriggle loose from Mama.

July 29 was Dorothy's birthday. That was only two weeks away.

Without Prince, Dorothy would not have reached her fourth birthday!

"*Be sober, be vigilant; because your adversary the devil, as a roaring (bull) . . . seek(s) whom he may devour . . .*"

Chapter 16. July 29, 1938

Watchie ... and the Mean Ol' Bull

Heading outside to do her morning chores, Katherine paused on the step of the open porch to view the shadowed yard. The sun was just rising over the barn.

In her mind's eye, Katherine still saw the threshing from last week. She pictured the humongous threshing machine and tractor in the open pasture behind the barn, where now only the straw pile remained.

She remembered especially the horses in the yard circling around and around to pull the shaft which activated the elevator to lift the oats. And she heard her terrified mother heading for Dorothy in the path of the circling horses.

Today was July 29, Dorothy's fourth birthday. How thankful she was that Dorothy was still alive to celebrate her birthday! Thankful to Prince and thankful to God.

Papa was not here this morning. He had to take his turns with threshing at neighboring farms. He had gone early so he could be home early.

Mama wanted to bake a birthday cake. They didn't always have birthday cakes. But Katherine understood Mama's need to do something special. She, too, was grateful.

*   *   *

All morning, Willie and Katherine rushed to get chores done alone. Since Papa wasn't home, Mama came out to help with milking. When she saw Willie and Katherine doing well without her, she went back inside.

And all morning, Katherine's mind struggled with one question. What could she do special for Dorothy? How could she show that she loved her?

At a loss, she finally asked Willie.

"Willie, Mama is baking Dorothy a cake. I think she has a present for her, too. Can you think of a birthday gift I could give her?"

Boys weren't much given to sentimentality . . . but Willie seemed to understand. He, too, had been touched by the incident with Dorothy and Prince.

"Let me think," he promised. "I'd kind of like to give her something, myself. Maybe you can help me think."

*   *   *

Katherine was delighted with the cake Mama made. It was a tall, marbled cake, with chocolate frosting. Mama had Katherine take it to the cool cellar.

To give Dorothy a special day, Mama gave all the children the afternoon off to play. This was a birthday present in itself.

"Mama, could we play on the straw pile?" asked Katherine. Ever since threshing, she had been itching to play on that wide, tall pile.

Mama hesitated. She didn't want straw scattered everywhere. But this was a special day. Finally she agreed.

"Why don't you wait awhile, though. Play by the crick while the sun is high. About an hour before chores' time, you can play on the straw."

"Dorothy loves the dirt piles that the horses made, Mama," Willie said. "Would it be okay if we let her play there, too, for awhile?"

Again Mama hesitated.

"Well, I guess she's going to be dirty, anyway, after playing in the crick and straw. But then she'll need a bath . . . and so will you. You must get in a little earlier. Can you do that?"

The children were delighted. They would have three special activities. First, playing by the crick. Second, playing in the horse-generated sand. And third, playing on the straw pile. What a wonderful afternoon!

*   *   *

Down by the river, Willie found his birthday present for Dorothy. He found three smooth stones with gray, beige and rose-colored layers. He polished them with his shirt and hid them in his pocket. Dorothy didn't notice.

Everyone had fun making a house and pig yard for Dorothy in the soft dirt from the horses. Dorothy loved it when Gerrit found sticks and called them little men, standing them inside the pretend pig yard. The stick men chased the pigs.

Willie found some funny-shaped corn cobs which became make-believe horses in a pasture. String from his pocket became harnesses on the horses. To make a pasture, he found sticks to become posts and tied string between the posts to become a fence. Horses must be fenced in, right?

Dorothy was too little to stay with one activity for long.

"Let's walk through the pasture," suggested Willie.

It was hot but a short walk would be fun, anyway. And Dorothy was happy with anything they suggested.

There were scads of flowers in the meadow. Wild onions had delicate white flowers. Near the ground were pinkish-white clovers and bluebells. Dorothy saw these flowers first. Willie and Katherine helped her pick some. She held them tightly, crushing them as she held them in her fist.

That was when Katherine decided her birthday gift. She would come back later and pick a fresh bouquet for Dorothy.

*   *   *

While they wandered through the meadow, the brown horses and Guernsey cows were all in the meadow as well. Prince, the horse who had saved Dorothy's life, nibbled meadow grass not too far away. It seemed to Katherine that he was still keeping a protective eye on Dorothy.

Their little dog, Watchie, had come with them into the meadow. Watchie was black and white, part Collie. He was a good cattle dog, kind with children.

Everyone liked the dog. Dorothy, especially, loved him. She would laugh and clap her hands whenever Watchie nuzzled her. "Puppy! Puppy!" she would exclaim. He stayed close by her the entire time they were in the meadow.

Watchie had gotten his name from what they *hoped* he would do. They expected him to be a watchdog. His job was to bark to alert them to strangers.

In the distance was a red bull with a white face. The bull was "a mean 'un", Papa said. Papa had gotten the bull at a bargain price and suspected the last owner was afraid of him. He did his job as a bull, so Papa kept him.

Willie and Dorothy had been warned to keep an eye on the bull. Since he was so far away, they weren't worried.

*   *   *

The sun was heading towards the horizon. It was time for the straw pile—the highlight of the day.

Climbing the straw pile was half the fun. The children scrambled up, slipping and falling. They tossed straw at each other in wild abandonment. Heedless of the noise, they laughed and squealed with glee. Willie and Katherine often stopped to help Dorothy. Gerrit made it to the top on his own.

Watchie headed for the house. It was cooler for him to lie in the shade of the big tree. He soon dozed off.

Reaching the top, the children lay in the straw and relaxed after the hot climb. Their energy revived when three of their neighbors, the Smidstras, came and joined them for the fun.

The children took turns coming up with games to play.

Willie led them in playing "King of the Mountain", which meant shoving each other down the sides of the pile while one person stood as king at the top. Since Willie was oldest, he usually was king.

Gerrit made up the next game. He tunneled through the straw from one side to the other like a wiggle worm, seeing who could get through the pile fastest. He won that game.

*   *   *

The seven children were laughing, giggling and shouting with such abandon, it never occurred to them to watch the meadow while they played. Why should they, anyway? The meadow was 'way far away!

Later, they wondered whether the noise they made was an irritant. Whatever the cause, a sudden blur of movement made them look towards the pasture . . . and freeze in fright.

Coming straight towards them at full run was the Mean Ol' Bull . . . "the Mean 'Un", as Papa called him. Its horns were lowered, its red coat glistening with sweat. Its eyes as they glared at the children were red with fury.

Frightened, the children screamed. Within seconds, Willie recovered and commanded the others, "Dig down into the straw. Keep quiet! Angry bulls don't like noise."

Quickly the others burrowed down out of sight.

Willie tried to distract the bull. He walked from one side to the other to confuse him, so he wouldn't know where to attack. The bull circled for awhile, watching Willie with those red eyes.

The distraction worked for a few minutes. Willie began to relax, thinking the bull would tire of the game and leave.

Suddenly the bull changed tactics completely. The bull lowered his horns and began to attack the straw. Straw, loosely piled up, flew every which way. The bull was trying to *climb* that pile to get at the children!

The children cringed with terror. The hidden children climbed back out of their burrows. They began to back down the opposite side from the bull, hoping he wouldn't notice, while Willie remained in open view.

For a minute, that seemed to work. They got halfway down before the bull circled the straw and saw them on that side. He again charged, tossing straw to get at them. The children's screaming only made him more furious.

Suddenly, Mama charged from the house. If the bull was furious, she was even more furious. Banging two pans together, she rushed to where Watchie was sleeping under the tree.

"Watchie, go get 'im! Sic' 'im!" Mama exclaimed. She continued banging the pans to distract the bull.

The small dog reacted immediately. Running swiftly, he nimbly nipped the bull on his hind heel . . . and danced away so the bull couldn't get him.

The bull turned its attention from the children to the dog. Roaring angrily, he turned and boxed at the dog. Watchie seemed to laugh at him, watching closely his every move.

As the bull lowered his head to charge him, Watchie changed location and again rushed the bull, nipping him this time on his left back leg. The bull again turned to attack him.

Meanwhile, the children backed from view on the opposite side of the pile. They hoped to get away before the bull noticed.

They didn't have to worry. Watchie was a natural cattle dog and instinctively knew what he was doing. He kept nipping the bull in just the right places to keep it moving. He himself was never in danger because he was much too agile for the bull to reach.

Before long, Watchie had the bull back in the pasture, running full speed to get away from the nipping dog.

That's when the other children bee-lined it for the safety of the house.

It wasn't too likely the bull would return.

*   *   *

Dorothy's party after supper was a very thankful party.

Everyone in the family marveled at what had happened. Twice in one week Dorothy had been saved by an animal! Once by a huge horse named Prince. Once by a small Collie dog named Watchie . . . Puppy, as she called him.

Papa had been told the story over and over.

Although he hadn't been there to see it, Papa promised to get rid of the bull. He would not have his family endangered by such an animal.

Watchie was duly rewarded. He was given a huge, meaty bone of the beef being served for supper. All the family petted him. It wasn't only Dorothy who hugged him; everyone did.

The dog may not have realized the reason but his wagging tail showed his love of all the attention. He had only done his duty. He had been a real watchdog . . . after Mama woke him up first.

And as for Dorothy's birthday?

Well, she really liked Willie's stones. She played with them all through supper. She only tried to bite them once.

Katherine had been too frightened to get the flowers. After Papa sold the Mean Ol' Bull—right away the next day—she picked a pretty bouquet . . . and Dorothy squealed with delight at receiving the flowers.

Gerrit, the budding artist, scribbled a picture for Dorothy. He drew the straw pile with the bull and dog at the bottom. You almost could recognize the dog nipping the bull's heels.

Dorothy fell asleep in the high chair before Mama could give her the cake. Mama had to save her a piece for the next day.

And Mama didn't give her present until Sunday.

Mama's gift was a new dress. She made it from a feed sack. It had on it a lovely bouquet of flowers, just like Katherine had picked. Mama had begun sewing it while the children were on the straw pile.

Mama's gift made Katherine giggle.

The same feed sack flowers were on some of her clothes. But while the flowers made a pretty dress for Dorothy, on Katherine they were underwear!

Chapter 17. Summer, 1938

Poison Ivy

"Whew! It must be one hundred degrees out here!"

It was the summer of 1938. The day was stifling hot. Temperatures were in the nineties. Eight-year-old Katherine dripped sweat from doing morning chores. She had helped Papa with yard chores and Mama with house chores.

All her thoughts now were on relaxing with a book. But . . .

"Willie and Katherine, go to the back pasture and pump water."

It was Papa talking. No one argued with Papa. Katherine only helped Mama when there was extra time after helping Papa. Outdoor chores were first.

"Papa, shall I wear overalls?" asked Katherine.

Girls always wore dresses around the house, even doing chores. But some chores merited overalls. This was an overalls' chore because she had to walk ¾ of a mile through tall, scratchy weeds to the back pasture.

"Yes, wear Willie's overalls," Papa responded. "You need not hurry. It's too hot. Be home for chores by the time the sun goes down.

"But, mind!" Papa added. "Even after the horses and cattle have drunk all they want, leave with the tank full of water."

Katherine's eyes shone. She would not need a book. True, the walk was long. Overalls made it even hotter. But it would be fun to relax by the creek. Willie would invent some fun.

*   *   *

By the time they reached the first creek, Katherine already regretted this chore. It was *so* hot! She brushed sweat from her face.

Willie and she stopped for two minutes by the first creek. They splashed water on their faces and arms to get rid of the sweat. It wouldn't help further on but felt good for a moment.

There were three pumps on the farm. The first was the *windmill* pump—water for the yard and house. The second was the *motor* pump—halfway across the first pasture, where the cows and four work horses grazed. The third was the *hand* pump—'way back in the second pasture. The same animals grazed back there when they wanted shady trees.

This far pasture had the creek winding through it a second time. Although they called it "the second creek", it was really the same creek after it had wound through a neighboring farm and then back again.

They were heading to the third pump, the second creek, the far pasture.

Mostly, they followed the wide paths the cows had made.

*   *   *

Katherine didn't like the smell of Willie's overalls. They smelled like barn. But smelly overalls were better than scratches.

The pastures were full of weeds. They walked through mustard, goldenrod, burdock and thistles . . . in addition to various pasture grasses. In hot weather, thistles multiplied overnight.

The government called thistles "noxious weeds". But Katherine loved the magenta color of the flowers.

"Willy, do you think I could have a dress the color of the thistle flowers?" Katherine asked whimsically. "It's so pretty!"

"You think thistles are pretty? Katherine, you silly!" Willie laughed at her. "Don't you know those flowers are seeds for new plants? If Papa didn't chop them, they'd cover the whole pasture. We'd have no place left to walk!"

Katherine knew that. She still thought magenta was pretty.

She tried to walk around the thistles. She was glad that the horses walked right over them, keeping the patches small.

Little finches loved thistle seed. When thistles were flowering, from a distance you could see the pretty, yellow and red breasted birds flitting around the flowers. It was their "steak dinner", Papa said.

Watching the finches was a treat for Katherine. She never tired of watching the little birds. Seventy years later—in a retirement home, a lady eighty years old—she would put thistle seed in hanging bird feeders and watch the finches flitting outside her window.

* * *

Once Willie and Katherine reached the second winding creek, they again stopped to cool off. This time there was no hurry. They lay in the grass by the creek and splashed water until they were completely cool.

Then it was time to pump water. The four brown horses—Frank, Molly, Topsy and Prince—were grazing nearby.

The pump was six feet from the round watering tank in the pasture. Papa had put a pipe from the pump to the six-foot tank so they didn't have to carry the water. At least that helped.

But pumping the handle was tiring. They had to take turns.

Willie pumped first. He primed it with a few pumps before water began to spurt out. Frank and Prince were so thirsty they slurped the water as soon as it spouted into the tank. Molly and Topsy kept grazing.

When Willie's arms became tired, Katherine pumped.

Pumping took a long time. Horses drink lots of water.

By the time they finished pumping, the children were swatting away little bugs, always attracted by sweat. They again needed to cool off by the creek.

* * *

Both Willie and Katherine took off their shoes. They waded along the creek to the wooden bridge which crossed the gravel road. The creek meandered under the bridge to the next farm.

Katherine rolled up Willie's overalls. She felt much cooler.

Neither Willie nor Katherine recognized a patch of plants by the creek. They seemed harmless. In spring, the three-pointed leaves were a pretty red color. Now they were a shiny green.

"Look at these leaves, Willie," Katherine said, pulling at his arm. "The outside leaves are gloves with one thumb pointed down."

Pausing to study the plants with her, Willie added, "You're right. And the middle leaf has two thumbs pointing up!"

Under the bridge, it was shady . . . a pleasant change from the hot sun in the pasture. Horses couldn't reach this spot because a wire fence stopped them.

Willie left his shoes near the plants, too, to keep dry. Now they could both wade in the water. Papa said that if your feet were cool, you felt cool all over. It was true. With feet in the cool water, Katherine's hot forehead felt cooler as well.

Once cooled off, Willie and she found little sticks to swirl the creek's water. That made the lazy, hidden creek life become active. Little minnows darted between weeds. Twice a water bug skimmed the surface. Once they spied a large carp—but it swam under the bridge when Willie tried to catch it.

For quite awhile, they had fun with small crabs. They were careful not to let the crabs catch hold of their fingers. But they teased them with sticks. They laughed when the crabs grabbed the sticks with their pinchers. Then they would swing them around until the crabs let go and flew into deeper water.

"Willie! What do you have there?" exclaimed Katherine. She had been busy watching the crabs and hadn't noticed him reaching behind them.

Willie grinned. "A toad!" he announced. "Think it'll stay in my pocket?"

Katherine's eyes were wide. "Won't you get warts?"

"Nah," scoffed Willy. "That's an old wives' tale!"

"What will Papa say?"

"He won't notice. If he does, he'll just tell me to drop it. It'll find its way back to the crick near the house."

*   *   *

They were having so much fun, they scarcely noticed the sun crossing the sky. But suddenly Willie did notice.

"Oops!" he said abruptly, pulling on his shoes as he talked. "We'd better high tail it home now. The sun's already over those trees."

Katherine was starting to itch. She quickly splashed water over her feet and arms to help the itch. Then she pushed through the three-leaved plants to a rock in the shade. There she pulled her shoes back on.

Meanwhile, Willie returned to the pump. He pumped another five minutes so they would leave the tank full of water. Katherine was glad she didn't have to pump again. She itched all over!

It didn't take more than five minutes of walking for all the coolness of the creek to feel lost. The heat made the itch worse, too.

"Katherine, can't you hurry?" Willie growled. Since they had left later than they should have, they had to make up for lost time.

"I'm trying, Willie, but I itch so bad!" Katherine replied. Looking at her, Willie saw that her skin was getting blotchy. He took her hand to help her walk.

"We'd better hurry faster, then," he responded logically. "Maybe Mama can help your itch."

*   *   *

By the time they reached the home creek, Katherine's itchiness had become unbearable. She didn't want to be a baby in front of Willie . . . but it was hard to hold back tears.

Papa met them at the top of the hill near the barn.

"I give you an afternoon off," he snapped, "and instead of watching the sun, you take advantage of me. Next time I'll tell you to come right home!"

Then he noticed Katherine's tears and saw her red, blotchy skin. The itchiness had spread over her whole body and was even going onto her face. Small blisters were beginning to form.

"Oh, no!" Papa moaned, shaking his head. "Were you two under the bridge? Have I never warned you of poison ivy? Katherine, leave it to you . . .

"I guess we'll have to do the chores alone, Willie. Katherine, you head for the house and see what Mama can do about your poison ivy."

*　*　*

Mama was instantly sympathetic.

"Girl! Girl!" she exclaimed. "What can we do? If only we had a shower, like some of the modern homes! Here, rinse yourself in the basin of water on the porch. I'll get a tubful of water for you to take a good bath."

Mama could certainly hurry. Within minutes, Katherine was soaking in a tepid tub of water . . . not too hot, because hot was the wrong thing for poison ivy, Mama said. Into the water she poured Baking Soda from a box she always kept handy. There were many uses for Baking Soda.

Katherine hadn't known a cool bath could feel that good. She kept dousing water all over her itchy red welts. Gradually, the itchiness subsided.

But the cool water, following the outdoor heat, had another result. Katherine began to shiver—first slightly, then violently.

Mama, seeing her shivering, felt Katherine's hot forehead.

"Oh my, Katherine," Mama moaned. "Why did you ever get into that poison ivy patch?" She shook her head and then answered herself, "I guess we just never warned you . . ."

Katherine felt so weak she could hardly get herself out of the tub and dressed. This time, she *wanted* a dress . . . no overalls to touch her skin!

It was too hot upstairs. It was also too hot in the kitchen, where Mama had been baking. Mama helped Katherine onto a mattress in the dining room. Still feverish, Katherine needed a light sheet around her despite the heat.

Mama made a paste of Baking Soda and covered all the itchy spots. It soothed the little blisters that were forming. Mama also gave Katherine a cup of cool tea. Usually she wasn't allowed tea; that was for adults.

Now there was no more Mama could think to do, so she went back into the kitchen to get supper on. Katherine closed her eyes and fell asleep. She slept all through chores' time.

*　*　*

Katherine was awakened by the gentle touch of Dorothy.

Four-year-old Dorothy had done Katherine's chicken chores. It was difficult for her but she was old enough and wanted to help.

"Are you any better?" asked Dorothy sympathetically.

Embarrassed over the entire episode, Katherine nodded her head. And indeed, she did feel better.

Mama saw Dorothy holding Katherine's hand. "Be careful!" she warned Dorothy. "Poison ivy is contagious. If the blisters pop, you could get it, too."

Katherine was able to get up and eat supper, although she still felt a bit dizzy . . . and itchy. The welts had gone down and weren't so red anymore. The blisters which had been forming were still there, however. Mama said blisters helped cool the skin. It was hard not to scratch them.

Papa was not angry anymore, and that helped. Thinking it over, he had realized that the children had not tried to do wrong. Coming home late had merely been a mistake.

"I think for a day or two, you'd better stay near the house, away from anything scratchy," he told Katherine. "You can help Mama with house jobs. Try to keep clean and cool until the itching is better. Otherwise, you can get infections. Then we'll have new problems."

Katherine was still embarrassed. But she was thankful, too. Thankful for Mama's bath and Baking Soda. Thankful for Papa's kindness right now. And especially thankful for a little sister who held her hand . . .

Even though the hand was covered with poison ivy blisters.

"*Precious memories, how they linger . . .*"

Chapter 18. May 27, 1940 Part 1

Memorial Day at Inspiration Hills

Grandpa and Grandma Tilstra's farm wasn't called Inspiration Hills in 1940. It was just the Tilstra Farm . . . the farm on which they raised their family of twelve children—the farm on which Mama Susie grew up. It became "Inspiration Hills" years later after it was sold.

In 1940, Grandpa and Grandma Tilstra still lived there with their youngest three boys, Uncles Bill, Pete and Dick. The long driveway to the house wound through pasture land. Parallel to the road but then veering to wind through the pasture was a railroad. Parallel to the driveway but across the pasture and down the hill was the Sioux River—a real river, not a creek, bordered by many large trees.

The Tilstra Farm was a beautiful location. Every Memorial Day, all the Tilstras gravitated back to the home place. Everyone loved the annual reunion.

* * *

"Papa, are we almost there?"

Papa chuckled. Katherine always asked that question.

Nine-year-old Katherine—seated between Willie and Gerrit with Dorothy in the front seat by her parents—could hardly wait for the four-year-old Model A Ford to finish climbing the long driveway through Grandpa and Grandma Tilstra's farm pasture. Peering through the car's side window, she could already see numerous vehicles parked around the large white farmhouse. Already her cousins were running around the house, playing tag. She couldn't wait to join them.

"Children," Mama's voice said sternly, "you must each carry something into the house." Without help, Mama would have to make several trips. Katherine was willing to help . . . but so eager to meet her cousins again!

Each of the married daughters and daughters-in-law took along something for the annual Tilstra Reunion. With all those hot dishes and desserts, there was no end to the good eating. Mama had made a delicious chicken hot dish with dumplings on top. She had also brought along two apple pies, made with apples still in the cold cellar from last year's crop.

The children scarcely waited for the car to stop.

"What should I carry, Mama?" Katherine waited impatiently, switching from foot to foot.

Willie carried Mama's hot dish. Katherine and Gerrit each carried one of the apple pies. Dorothy carried a package of Mama's rolls. Papa and Mama took everything else. They carefully walked up the wide steps of the white farmhouse porch . . . and almost dropped what they were carrying when aunts rushed out to meet them with endless hugs. "Oh my, look how she has grown . . . !"

"And just think, next week she will be ten years old already!"

*　　*　　*

"When do we eat?" queried Gerrit. After all, it was already 10:00 . . . and breakfast had been two hours ago . . .

Mama Susie chuckled. "Here's two cookies and some water to help you wait, Gerrit," she responded. She had taken along several dozen cookies, knowing how hungry boys always were. This was not a day to practice self-control.

The cousins, seeing Gerrit with cookies, scampered to the porch to join him. Soon all the boys were munching cookies and drinking water. The girls followed suit. Three dozen cookies were gone in minutes.

"Children," Grandpa Tilstra grinned, perching on the porch railing, "would you like to go play across the road? There's that hill across the road that you always like to climb. Are you ready for it?"

"Yippee!" exclaimed Gerrit, remembering from last year. He was ready to dash that way immediately.

"Hold it a minute," Grandpa said before anyone got away. "We must remember the rules first. What three things mayn't you do? Who remembers?"

Willie chimed up with Rule 1. "Stay away from the train track! You never know when a train may come through!"

Cousin Augusta said Rule 2. "Stay away from the river!" The Sioux was a large river. It could be dangerous for the little children.

That emboldened Katherine to chant Rule 3. "Stay away from the horse!" Grandpa had a large stud in a big corral. He did not want any children to get the horse excited.

"We'll *stay away* from all three things," the children called out. And before anything more could be said, they were off and running across the pasture land towards the railroad and road, pausing to make sure no train or cars were coming before they crossed.

* * *

"Hey, Augusta, I'll beat you to the top!"

It was so much fun, climbing up and down that sand hill. It was, of course, all the cousins that made it fun. Katherine was especially close to Cousin Augusta, who was almost her age.

Katherine recalled the time she and Augusta had become friends. Augusta had spent a whole week at their Rock Rapids' home. Shortly before that visit, Mama had bought Katherine a rare gift, a new pair of white shoes for Sunday. Augusta had loved those new shoes.

One day during that week, a bad summer storm had come up. Papa had said, "Everyone, time to go in the cellar." As they headed down, Augusta stopped Katherine and said, "Be sure to take your new shoes along, Katherine!"

To both of them, anything new was considered precious.

* * *

Climbing the sand hill, Katherine's legs soon began to tire.

After her fifth climb up the hill, she lay down in a shady spot and just gazed around at the scenery. She loved looking towards the Sioux River. If it wasn't a rule, how she would have loved to walk down there among the trees! She knew there would be lots to explore there. But rules were rules, sigh.

Augusta sat down next to Katherine.

"Wouldn't it be great to explore the river?" she asked wistfully. "I wouldn't dare today, but sometime, maybe . . . ?"

Katherine sighed. "Yeah, but, you know, we never get to be here except when all the family is here. There'll never be a chance to explore it with just the two of us. Never, never!"

"Oh, listen!" exclaimed Augusta. "Hear that?"

With all the excited shouting around them, it took a minute to hear. By then all the children stopped what they were doing to listen. Sure enough, they could hear a train whistle in the distance, coming closer with each second. The train whistled a warning every time it approached a road of any kind.

"The train! The train!" exclaimed Dorothy, now nearly four years old. She was jumping up and down in place.

Five-year-old Gerrit was just as excited. "I see its smoke!" he exclaimed, pointing. Everyone could see its smoke as it curled its way around the hills. Mostly the train track would parallel the road.

Another half minute and the train came into view. First they saw the large engine with its smokestack. The train was right across the road and they were all watching it, so the engineer saw them. He waved and blew the whistle for them.

The train had numerous cars carrying cargo. The boys began chanting as they counted cars. "Fifty . . . Fifty-one . . . Fifty-two . . ." They could hardly count fast enough to keep up, the train was moving so swiftly. "Fifty-three!!" they all said together as the caboose rolled past.

"Aw-w-w," whined Gerrit, "I thought there were one hundred at least."

"It was SO MUCH FUN!" responded Dorothy, a smile from one ear to the next. "I want to go tell Papa!"

The grownups were already watching from the house, ready for the children to come back. It was noon now and their stomachs were growling.

* * *

All too soon, the delicious food was only a memory. Katherine's stomach was deliciously full . . . much too full to go running again. Each of the girls helped carry dishes and food to the kitchen but then the grownup women took over doing dishes.

Katherine and Augusta sat on the grass by the wide steps, content to relax and listen to the adults visiting on the wide veranda. Closest to where they sat were Grandpa and Papa. Katherine could hear everything they said.

Grandpa Tilstra said, "Grandma and I both lived in the United States all our lives; we are second-generation Dutch. But Wilbur, here, immigrated from the Netherlands himself; he's first-generation Dutch. Tell us your story, Wilbur."

Wilbur looked into the distance. You could see him thinking hard about his home across the ocean.

"My parents in the Netherlands were wonderful parents," he said after a pause. "But we were seven boys, no girls. Our land was just a small plot. There was no way we could all earn a living on that land. Life was hard. So three of us chose to leave and come to America, not expecting a Depression here.

"First Will and John came. They both started out in North Dakota, but John soon left for Washington and, after the Black Blizzards, Will followed him. I came to America later . . . but I'm the only one in Iowa."

Grandpa nodded. He knew most of Papa's story.

"Have you heard from your brothers since Will moved to Washington?" he asked. "What was that, four years ago?"

Papa nodded. "Yes, it will be four years ago this summer," he responded. "From Ann's letters, I'd say it has gone well. Both brothers are into dairy farming now, along with crops. Washington has good land and good moisture . . . and they are doing well."

Katherine sighed happily. She was so glad it had turned out well. She could never forget the Black Blizzard. She had been so afraid for her cousins, Willie and Tillie. She hoped someday she could see them again.

* * *

It was so pleasant here! Lying on the grassy slope by the porch, one hand holding onto Augusta's hand, Katherine stared into the wide Memorial Day sky.

Memorial Day: a day for remembering. For remembering those who had died for the country. But also for other memories. Listening to the talk on the porch brought those memories to life . . .

And added new memories . . .

"*If I Gain the World . . . but lose the Savior*"

Chapter 19. Memorial Day 1940, Part 2

Remembering . . . and Looking Forward

For awhile, Katherine forgot about the men on the porch. She was thinking about the Depression years and her father's brothers. They had been difficult years, but . . . now Uncles Will and John were doing well in Washington.

Grandpa Tilstra was still talking with Papa.

"These Depression years have been tough," Grandpa said. "Sometimes the Depression made it hard to stay healthy, wouldn't you say, Wilbur?"

Papa hesitated before answering.

"Well, I don't know," he countered. "We had to raise our own food, and, you know, that was healthy. Don't you agree that all the fresh garden produce, though lots of work to grow, is both delicious and healthy?

"But we certainly didn't have money to spend on doctors and dentists."

Papa had a far-away look on his face. Katherine knew a story was coming. She leaned forward to listen.

* * *

"I remember one Sunday in the fall of 1935. Coming home from church, Willie complained of a headache. Susie felt his forehead. He was burning

with fever. Susie sent me right back to Rock Rapids for Dr. Corcran. He came immediately, even though he knew we didn't have much money.

"Willie had pneumonia. Seriously ill. We thought we'd lose him.

"Dr. Corcran came that day and several more times. Every time he came, he brought a treat for the kids. Not just a piece of worthless candy, but fruit. He didn't have to do that but he wanted to see the kids healthy.

"We saw it as the love of God shining through a doctor. He couldn't have shown that love if we were wealthy. You don't see doctors today doing that!"

*   *   *

Grandpa nodded. "Yes, I think the Depression can be an opportunity for real good in many ways. But there still were hardships. Didn't Susie lose a baby a few years ago?"

Papa nodded his head, and Katherine, glancing up, was surprised to see sudden tears fill his eyes. Mama had told her the story but she hadn't known Papa felt it so much.

"It happened on February 23, 1936, four years ago," Papa said softly. "Susie was carrying a baby boy who was due any day. It was icy outside but she needed water and went out to the windmill. Somehow the water splashed, causing her to slip on a slab of ice and to fall. She went into labor the next day.

"We might have been able to save the baby if we had owned a telephone. Without a phone, we couldn't call the doctor, so we had no help.

"It was a harsh winter, too much snow to get the doctor and too cold to bury the baby. I made a box for the child. Susie gave me a soft blanket to wrap the body. We put him in the empty chicken house until spring. After the ground thawed, we buried the boy in the Rock Rapids' cemetery. We marked his plot with a simple wooden cross."

Papa added, "We haven't had another child since then."

*   *   *

"I'm sorry, Wilbur. I shouldn't have asked you about that," Grandpa said softly, placing a hand on Wilbur's arm. "I was just thinking how the Depression causes serious losses, too."

Papa nodded, then smiled. "You know, there are good things to remember, too, about the Depression. Lots of them, really.

"I think of the poor bums who rode the trains, looking for income. They were homeless due to the Depression. They would look for a meal, not just a handout but willing to work for a meal. Of course, any Christian person was happy to help them, knowing they were honest men, just desperately poor. Some of them still had families at home.

"The fun part was that these railroad bums had their own code. They invented an open sun for a generous family, a darkened circle for a crabby wife. When they visited a kind home, they would make this sun on the fence posts.

"I consider it a badge of honor to have that circular sun on our posts. I'll never, ever, remove those posts from our land! They are souvenirs for me."

*   *   *

Grandpa, with his own memories, began chuckling.

"Remember that we earlier talked about Susie going to help my brother, her Uncle Fred Tilstra?" he asked.

Papa wondered why Grandpa smiled. It seemed solemn, not a joke.

"Well, these twin brothers—my twin brother and I—certainly populated a lot of Iowa!" he chortled. "There are Tilstras scattered all over the area. From the three sons of my brother, the whole Steen area has Tilstras. From the seven boys of the other twin, myself, there are Tilstras in Steen, Inwood, Canton, Rock Rapids, Hull, Rock Valley and Hills . . . and several other towns. Not to mention the families of the married daughters, like the Kroontjes!"

*   *   *

"Uh, Wilbur, how do you answer your children when they ask you where babies come from?" asked Grandpa. He winked at the girls.

"Well, you know, that's kind of a hush-hush thing," Papa grinned back. "Once Susie said babies came from the cabbage patch!"

By then the ladies, finished with dishes, were joining the men on the porch. Mama Susie heard Papa and laughed merrily.

"Another time I told Gerrit, 'The doctor brings babies in his black bag.'"

Papa laughed, "I don't think you ever told the same fiction twice, Susie."

Grandpa nodded. "My wife always made up some answer, too, so Susie comes by her evasions naturally.

"But I can't quite see, myself, why evasion is necessary. Why not just say that God gives the babies? That's true . . . and isn't that enough?"

Papa nodded. "We can just quote *Psalm 127*, can't we? '*Lo, children are a blessing of the LORD.*'"

*   *   *

"Your hard work has paid off, Son," Grandpa said to Papa. Katherine knew Papa was Grandpa's son-in-law, but Grandpa Tilstra was showing that he thought of Papa as a son. "You may not be wealthy but you have survived the worst Depression years. Slowly, slowly, you are gaining ground. It will be worth it all in the future; you will see."

Papa was thoughtful.

"I think you are right," he responded. "The children are learning to work, for one thing, which would not be so necessary if we were wealthy."

"Another good lesson," joined in Uncle Walt, "is to be content with small pleasures. Look at the fun your kids have for hours with homemade games. They have more fun than rich kids with $100 toys that mean nothing."

Katherine thought about the games they invented at home. She remembered Dorothy's birthday. They had played for hours making up their little farm with sticks that were pretend horses and other sticks that were pretend fences. What fun it had been!

Or, look at the hours spent on the straw pile.

Or, just now, the fun on that sand piled across the road.

Yes, Uncle Walt was right. Poverty brought out the imagination. And pretending was fun. Without store-bought toys, they had always had fun.

*   *   *

Papa suddenly grinned again as he looked at Katherine.

"Talk about having homespun fun," he chuckled. "I remember a little girl who once had fun with corn cobs and kerosene. Remember that, Katherine?"

Katherine blushed. She hung her head and said nothing.

Mama was still on the porch. The ladies were all looking at photographs. Mama was looking at one of Willie and Katherine.

"Wilbur!" she chided gently. "It wasn't her fault. She was just a baby. If anything, we learned some valued lessons about the worth of our children."

Papa looked lovingly at the mother. "You are right as usual, Susie," he responded. "And I think you have proof right there in your hands. Isn't that the photograph we took a few months after Katherine drank that kerosene?"

"Yes," Mama nodded. "We were so thankful still to have both children. We were reminded how easily we can lose them. When a photographer came around, we couldn't resist having a photograph taken of the children. We went to Rock Rapids to get them taken. Don't you think he did a nice job?"

As the photograph made the rounds, everyone agreed. That photograph was a wonderful memento and a great reminder. Life was a gift of God.

Every life. Every day.

*   *   *

"What do you think of the turmoil going on in Europe right now?" Uncle Bill suddenly asked, changing the topic. "Do you think the United States is going to get involved in all this?"

Grandpa looked serious.

"That Hitler has sure got all the German people following him," he responded. "He goes from one thing to the next. Conquering Austria, acting like they deserved it. Rounding up the Jews, acting like they deserved it. Conquering Poland, acting like they deserved it. I think he wants to conquer the world."

"Yeah," Uncle Bill added, "and now Italy has joined with Germany, acting just as crazy. That's a powerful coalition."

Papa agreed. "I don't see that we will be able to stay out of that war. If God gives us men who can fight, I think we'll have to sacrifice in order to stop that German maniac."

"Lots of Americans don't want to see us at war, though," argued Uncle Bill. "They think that it's a war across the ocean and doesn't involve us. They say we have an *isolationist* policy."

Katherine looked at Uncle Bill. He was just the age when young men would go to war. She wondered if he would volunteer. Or Uncles Walt, Pete or Dick. Any of them could join the military.

"Well, we'll have to wait and see what the government decides," responded Grandpa soberly. "Myself, I think that it's high time we start helping. After all, it's Wilbur's family that is suffering in the Netherlands right now."

Katherine hadn't thought about that before. Papa's mom and dad were over there, too. They were under Hitler's armies. Of course they must help!

Even if it meant that her uncles might go to war, too.

*　　*　　*

The sun was dropping now towards the western horizon over the trees. It was nearly time for the families to head home.

Grandma Tilstra brought out homemade ice cream. The aunts scooped it into bowls for everyone's final treat. Grandma would wash these bowls while they were on their ride home.

The three younger Tilstra sons—Bill, Pete and Dick—came out of the house with instruments. These brothers had become fairly good with guitars, fiddles and banjos. Their music made Katherine's feet itch to move with the beat.

The three brothers played a variety of music, all by ear. They were especially good at country western music, the kind often heard on radio programs.

Katherine knew some of the fun songs by Stephen Foster, because Papa also sang them for fun. "*Camptown Races*" was a song from her red school music book. *"I went down south for to see my gal . . ."* The uncles sang the story parts while everyone sang the refrain, "*Doo—dah! Doo—dah!*"

After nearly half an hour of playing fun style music, the uncles switched to psalms and hymns, music they knew the parents loved best. Everyone sang along on the hymns.

Katherine thought the singing was better than the best choir. She loved Papa's deep voice and Mama's sweet contralto. The sound of all those uncles singing made her tingle all over.

Long after the day ended, after she was back home and nearly asleep, Katherine could still hear in her mind the lively music of the fiddles, played while the sun was setting.

"If I gained the world but lost the Savior,
Were my life worth living for a day?
Could my yearning heart find rest and comfort
In the things that soon must pass away?

"Oh! The joy of having all in Jesus!
What a balm the broken heart to heal!
Not a sin so great but He'll forgive it;
Not a sorrow that He does not feel.

"If I have but Jesus, only Jesus,
Nothing else in all the world beside,
Oh! Then all I need I have, in Jesus!
For my needs and more He will supply."

Such singing, she thought, must be one of the wonderful things about heaven. As long as there was music, she wouldn't trade places with anyone in the world.

Chapter 20. November 11, 1940

Blizzard of the Century

No one, but no one, realized that November 11, 1940, would be a history-changing day. Not even the meteorologists. And they should have known. It was their job to know.

But, what meteorologists?

The only meteorologists were in Chicago . . . and they weren't even in the building the night before that day!

*　　*　　*

November 11, 1940: Armistice Day. A day to remember the peace treaty which ended World War I. Later its name became Veterans' Day.

November 11, 1918, was a day which people still remembered in 1940.

In school, Katherine's teacher discussed the day. How important it was that everyone should try to keep their promises—promises to keep peace.

But how Germany, the same country which had started World War I, was now starting another world war. World War II.

The students all shivered a bit, thinking about another world war.

*   *   *

Armistice Day, 1940, started out as a beautiful fall day.

"I've never seen such a lovely fall," Mama said. "Day after day of gorgeous weather. My, I am getting so many things done this fall."

"Yes," Jennie Kracht replied, "Ma hasn't even cooped up the chickens."

Everyone marveled at the weather. Not a single frost yet!

*   *   *

It was hard for Katherine to sit still in school.

It was harder for the boys. Sixty degrees! Shouldn't they be outdoors?

Young and old, men were all hunting that day. Never, in the history of the Midwest, had so many men all decided on the same day to go hunting.

And, why not? Fall work was finished. The weather was incredible! And overhead, humongous groups of birds were flying eastward. It was tantalizing.

Birds swooped towards lakes at 90 miles per hour. It was unreal.

Yet no one, but no one, thought of the mass migrations as a warning. They saw the flocks of birds as a beckoning. A beckoning to hunt.

*   *   *

Hunters who reached the lakes early saw a strange sight.

Birds settled on the lakes in huge flocks. There were so many birds that at first the hunters didn't realize they were there. They had their heads down, neck to neck, as if they were forming a huge blanket for mutual protection. Hunters couldn't even see water.

Once the hunters realized what they were seeing—that these were all birds, birds, birds, neck to neck—they began shooting. Bird after bird after bird.

And the crazy birds never even flew away! They just stayed right there, heads down, shoulder to shoulder, and let men shoot!

Were the birds crazy?

Or . . . were the men crazy who didn't heed the birds' warning?

*   *   *

Although wind began howling in early afternoon, at first no one paid attention. The temp' was sixty degrees. So what if there was a little wind?

Then it began to rain. Before long the rain changed to sleet and ice. Snowflakes began.

Katherine felt the change in atmosphere. Everyone in school kept glancing at the window, surprised by the sudden howling of the wind, by how quickly snow began to swirl. Within an hour it was a blizzard.

The Armistice Day Blizzard of 1940. The Blizzard of the Century.

The blizzard that would change meteorology.

*   *   *

Miss Sands was also watching the sky. When the winds began, she continued teaching. She continued teaching as the rain began. As sleet began.

When the snow began, a frown gathered on Miss Sands' forehead. All the children became very quiet, wondering what she would do.

The change from sun to wind to rain to sleet to snow happened within one class period. Before Miss Sands had time to form a plan, it was already too late. Wind whipped around the building and the windows, darkened with sudden blizzard. Quietly, Miss Sands ended the school day. She led in closing prayer and organized the children to go home. Most of them didn't even have good coats because they hadn't known they would need winter protection.

The Smidstra children lived close to school. It seemed safe to let them walk home. Miss Sands wrapped towels around their heads to protect them, since they had no winter caps. (Why were those towels in the school, anyway?)

Miss Sands looked worried. Should she have let the Smidstras go?

Katherine felt worried. Would other parents get to them on time?

*   *   *

Due to the wind, no one heard the knock. They jumped when the door suddenly flew open. Katherine nearly shouted for joy. There was Papa!

"Quickly, Willie and Katherine, Gerrit and Dorothy. We have to get home to save the livestock!" Papa did not smile.

Right behind Papa were other farmers. In that short time, the snow was already inches thick. Everyone arrived with horses pulling sleighs.

Katherine had to fight the wind to get into the sleigh. Once there, she huddled with Dorothy and Gerrit under the blanket in the bottom.

*   *   *

They had made it! They were home and safe!

"Willie," Papa shouted above the noise of the storm, "don't change clothes. I need you to help me round up the cattle before they die in this storm. I already got the hogs into the hog building. We need both of us to get the cows and horses into the barn.

"Mom is outside with Jennie, trying to round up chickens. They were roosting in the trees, crazy birds.

"I don't want any of the rest of you outside. It's too easy to get lost and die in a blizzard. Stay put, you hear?"

The children nodded, too subdued to say anything.

With Mama and Jennie outside, Katherine was the oldest person in the house. She gave everyone cookies and milk, their usual after-school snack.

Then everyone joined her at the window, watching that sudden storm. Were Mama and Jennie safe? Were Papa and Willie okay?

*   *   *

It seemed forever until the door whipped open and Mama and Jennie blew back into the house. Both of them were as white as snowmen—snow on their hair, under their scarves, over their faces and coats and shoes. Mama's tongue was out, licking snow off her upper lips. Her nose was frosty. Jennie was brushing snow off her eyes and eyebrows so she could see again.

But they were safe!

Papa and Willie weren't far behind Mama and Jennie.

Outside, they couldn't see one step in front of them. If they had been out any longer, they would never have found their way back into the house. And the warm temperatures had turned fiercely cold.

178

Papa and Mama were both breathing hard. Mama's nose was bright red.

Katherine quickly got out cups and poured hot coffee for all five of them. Even Willie was allowed coffee to warm himself up.

Before long, Jennie caught her breath enough to begin helping Katherine. A pot of hearty pea soup was already simmering on the stove. While Dorothy set the table, Jennie ladled out the soup and everyone sat down for supper.

It was too noisy for Papa to read devotions. He only led them in prayer, which they had to strain to hear. But the routine was comforting, anyway.

With the static of the radio joining the howl of the wind, everyone was ready for stories. And they heard them! For weeks afterwards, they heard stories!

*   *   *

Mama's story was first.

"I have never seen such crazy birds!" she exclaimed. "They were all in the trees. Chickens in the trees! Have you ever . . . ?"

Shaking her head, Mama continued.

"But do you think we could get them out? My, what a work! They were so spooked, they were like they were crazy. Just wanted to huddle in those trees! They would all have died out there.

"It was all Jennie and I could do to get them down. If we left them alone, they would fly right back up into the trees. One by one, we had to catch them and bring them to the chicken coop. One by one.

"It's like they knew this would be a blizzard. Like they knew that if they stayed on the ground, the snow would cover them and kill them.

"I've never seen anything like it!"

*   *   *

With the extreme winds outdoors, the house had become cold as well. Even though it had been winterized with tar paper and hay bales, the small house was no match for those howling winds. Pipes from the stoves in the kitchen and dining room rattled and shook as the wind howled down them.

Everyone wore coats in the house!

Mama wrapped blankets around the children.

Everyone sat on chairs as close to the stove as they dared.

Except Papa. He sat by the radio, trying different stations, listening to the static and trying to make out what the announcers were saying.

But finally he gave up, also. He simply couldn't hear anything.

*　　*　　*

Long before bedtime, Papa and Mama sent everyone up to bed.

Katherine wished she could light the kerosene lantern and read awhile. But with the wind swirling through the cracks in the house, she didn't dare. She could start a fire.

Late into the night she lay there, just listening. Unable to sleep.

But feeling warm and safe in bed was better than sitting downstairs and shivering. No one could talk much, anyway, with all that howling noise.

*　　*　　*

After the blizzard was over, they heard more stories.

One hunter said the sky turned orange as the blizzard approached.

Hunters everywhere had been caught by the blizzard. They had been unprepared, many of them dressed only in short-sleeved shirts. The weather had been that beautiful in the morning. Sixty degrees in the early afternoon.

Along the Mississippi River, especially, many hunters had died. Some had drowned as they tried to make it to shore through huge waves in the sudden cold. Others had tried to find shelter on islands but their shelters were destroyed by cyclonic winds and gigantic waves. Without warm clothes, they froze during the night in the unexpected, bitter cold.

One teen-aged boy on an island jumped all night. His legs froze and needed to be amputated. His older brother froze to death right next to him.

In Minnesota, 49 people died. Half of them were duck hunters.

Two trains collided in Watkins, Minnesota, killing two passengers.

On Lake Michigan, 59 sailors died on three freighters. Huge waves had caused the freighters to capsize.

13 people died in Illinois, 13 in Wisconsin and 4 in Michigan.

Altogether, 160 people died in the thousand-mile wide blizzard.

In Iowa, twenty foot drifts covered vehicles and made roadways impassable. Thousands of Iowa cattle and more than a million Thanksgiving turkeys died.

Katherine later read an official Iowa report. *"It is remembered as the day the winds descended, the heavens rained ducks, and duck hunters died."*

*   *   *

Meteorologists were haunted. They had not forecast anything at all. Listeners were stunned. How could these men pretend they were forecasting weather events when something like this blizzard was not forecast at all?

All the meteorologists could do was apologize. What could they say? They hadn't known! And they had to admit, they needed to improve.

To their credit, they did improve. Forecasting has never been the same. Dedicated meteorology began with this blizzard. Study of weather became a science. Today's forecasts are much, much more reliable.

All because of the Armistice Day Blizzard of 1940.

*   *   *

In the morning, the house was much warmer . . . but was dark as night. Snow had piled up around the house, creating a cocoon. Snow totally hid the windows. The wind still howled down the pipes of the stoves but that was the only place it could enter the house.

Papa and Willie couldn't even get to the barn in the morning. They had to hope the animals were okay.

In the afternoon, the blizzard let up and the men managed to get outside. There were such piles of snow, there was still no way to get into the buildings. They had to dig tunnels through the snow. The younger children stayed in the house while Papa and Willie dug the way to the buildings.

That first day, Katherine never ventured outside. Mama wouldn't allow it.

The second day, she was able to do her chores again. But she had to walk through tunnels Papa and Willie had dug.

In fact, they had to keep using those tunnels for weeks. The car was stuck in the garage with no way to get it out. Papa and the neighbors took turns going to town for necessities, using horses and the sleigh. There was no church.

They remained snowed in for the rest of 1940. Even for Christmas.

It wasn't until January that there was a thaw. Finally, they were able to open the buildings and get the car out.

*　　*　　*

About a week after the blizzard, a knock sounded on the door. There stood Mr. Smidstra! His nose was red, he was breathing hard, but he was smiling.

And the sun was shining, even though it was bitterly cold.

"Neighbor!" boomed Papa's voice. "Welcome! Come in for coffee."

"Ah-h-h . . . Wonderful!" Mr. Smidstra relaxed in one of Mama's wooden kitchen chairs. He closed his eyes, relishing the warmth of the coffee.

"And what brings you here on this lovely . . . uh . . . cold winter day?" Papa's eyes twinkled as he stumbled over his words.

"Well," Mr. Smidstra admitted, "I really just had to get away for awhile. The kids have been driving me nuts. My wife can handle it; I needed a break.

"So I decided to find out if you think we can get the kids back into school. Your buildings are snowed in yet, so you can't drive the children to school. But do you think it's safe for them to walk?"

Papa looked serious. "Neighbor, you live close by the school and your children could walk. But mine couldn't. There are huge drifts piled everywhere. They couldn't walk a fourth of a mile in this snow!"

"Yeah," Mr. Smidstra replied, "I've thought about that danger. I agree. But I really think the children should be in school, too.

"Here's my solution.

"First, we as neighbors could all get together and pull the children to school on home-made sleighs. Put runners under farm wagons and turn them into temporary sleighs, right? We all have horses to pull them.

"Second, if another blizzard should blow up, Miss Sands will have to use her judgment to do one of two things. Either everyone can stay put in school until we can get there. Or else they can all hold hands together and walk to our place. We have enough room to manage until it's possible to go home."

Papa rubbed his chin thoughtfully.

"Education is mighty important," he agreed. "We can't live our lives doing nothing because maybe something could go wrong.

"Mighty good of you to offer your place for food and a shelter. With that solution, I think we should open the school again."

And so, a week after the blizzard, with tunnels still providing the only way into the barns, the children bundled up and rode on wagon-sleighs to school.

Katherine's heart was glad. She was no longer snowbound!

And if another blizzard came?

Why, she'd simply sleep with Jessie! Jessie, her best friend.

No, second-best. Because God was her best friend. He was always there.

Postlude #1 To Our Readers

What a year this has been!

For someone who has always wanted to write, the past eleven months of writing collaboration with Katherine have been a dream come true. Katherine not only has stories to tell, she also is very detail conscious. She is willing to go over and over things so that this very fallible writer can finally get it right. She is ready to go through her own large collection of memorabilia and find things to illustrate her stories . . . not only for illustrations in the book but for me, the writer, so that I understand. Details to her are real life. She has lived them.

Note that the writing of the first book took only eleven months. We began expecting to take one year and to write one book with Katherine's entire life story. Within two months of our collaboration, we realized that one book would not suffice. So our plan is revised. If God permits, we now plan a series of three books, one for each of Katherine's childhood homes.

For a scholar, this writing has also been an opportunity for research. I now understand more of the Depression years than ever before. My library now includes several new books on the Depression years. Old but valuable books in my own library, which I seldom looked at before, are now thumb-eared. Internet research has been extensive. I have never considered myself an expert in the department of history; nor would I now; but in this era of the Depression, I would now be able to teach the history with much more charisma.

Until one tries to write a book, it is impossible to realize how many revisions writing entails. Our completed first manuscript, on typing paper, includes nearly 200 pages. There are five hundred sheets of paper in a ream of paper. How many reams do you think we used in writing this book? Not one. Not two. Not three or four. Eight! Eight reams of paper . . . or 4,000 sheets! I have emptied my garbage pail many, many times. To conserve trees, we recycled the used paper.

It is all worth it. Our first book of memories is complete.

Remember that this remains a fictional biography. We have tried very hard to make all the facts correct so that Katherine's relatives can learn accurate facts. We hope the average reader can gain a true picture of Katherine's Depression years in Iowa. Yet the conversations, some scenarios, and some observations—needed to create readability—remain fictional.

Now we begin all over again. For Katherine's story is only begun. Some of her most interesting memoirs are yet to come. I can't wait to get into them . . .

Carol Brands, July 3, 2009

Postlude #2 by Katherine

I have for many years enjoyed reading through books of the "olden days".

When I moved into this retirement home two years ago, my children couldn't understand why I wanted to take with me all my books of memories. I took along with me my photo albums. My *SEARS'* catalogue from 1904 (before I was even born). My expensive set of **Good Old Days** books. My scrapbook of World War II, made while I was a teenager. The music lesson books which I used to learn to play piano. My *Little Red Music Book* from first grade. And many other sentimental books.

Not to mention so many other things! A host of videos. A variety of music books. Crocheting books . . . and crocheted items for give-away. Wall hangings and other treasured keepsakes . . .

I just couldn't part with them. They were a part of me.

I also couldn't part with my memories.

So often my mind was reviewing the memories of my life. When workers were helping me, I would tell stories about which I was always thinking. Memories. Precious memories.

To several of these workers, I commented, "My life should be put in a book." I really felt that way. There were so many interesting stories. The children of today should understand what life was like before modernization.

I want my own children to know these stories. My own grandchildren.

That's why I appreciated working with Carol Brands, a special CNA who entered my life after I moved here. I am so thankful that she likes to write and was willing to write my stories.

We hope that all of you readers—not just my children, grandchildren, siblings, nephews and nieces—will be able to enjoy these stories.

And we hope that through them you can learn what we learned. No matter what trials life brings, always trust God. He knows the end from the beginning. He uses all our trials to bring us closer to Him.

That is my prayer as we end the writing of this first book and send it out to a publisher. May God use this book to help you, the reader, and for His glory.

Katherine Kroontje Vastenhout, July 3, 2009

Postlude #3 For the Historical Record

If you merely read this book for pleasure, great! That is mostly how I read books. Then don't read this postlude. It will be boring for you.

If, however, you are reading just as much to learn facts, you need this postlude. It tells you how much you can trust what you have read.

Chapter 1. Factual: the setting of Katherine's birth and all information about her parents.

Chapters 2-3. Factual: The Corn Cob incident—drinking the kerosene and trip to doctor. Details surrounding the incident are real memories of normal daily life inserted at this point.

Chapter 4. Accurate: Mama's Sears' order; Daddy's Model A Ford and its description; family life details. Papa and Mama's disagreement is fictional.

Chapter 5. Accurate: the detailed memories and fears of the Gypsy visit . . . all except narrative.

Chapter 6. Setting and facts are all accurate. "Mama's Tears" are fictional.

Chapters 7-8. Accurate: the description of the "Black Blizzard" and the population shift away from the Dakotas; the necessity of farmers to slaughter animals; the Willie and Tillie facts; the trip and taking along chickens plus produce. Invented are Road Numbers; they didn't exist in those days. Also, while they were thin, the N.D. Kroontjes weren't "sticks and bones".

Chapter 9. Accurate: description of the school, clothes, lunchpail, books, students, school day, and friendship with Jessie. We realized later that Miss Sands was teacher when Dorothy began school, Miss Orla Guik when Katherine began. Note that "under God" was added to the Pledge in 1954.

Chapter 10. Accurate: Katherine's mothering of Dorothy; Gerrit's birth and Katherine's comment; Dorothy's metal crib; Katherine's corncob mattress; cleaning windows and banking the house.

Chapter 11. Everything about the whooping cough and Dr. Corcran is accurate.

Chapters 12-13. Accurate is the description of Tony and his obsession with his bicycle. Unknown is the kind of bicycle. Accurate is the description of the radio, its purchase, its installation, and the favorite programs. Accurate is the lightning strike, the tree splinters, and the sulfur incident.

Chapters 14-16. Every detail related to threshing is accurate—except Katherine may have been a year or two older when she set up the oat bundles. The scenario with Dorothy and Prince is accurate. The straw pile with the "Mean Ol' Bull" and Watchie is accurate—except Dorothy questions whether she was on the pile, thinks she was in the house with Mama.

Chapter 17. The entire setting and the poison ivy are accurate, as are Mama's remedies.

Chapters 18-19. All details of the setting are accurate. The scenario on the sand pile is accurate. The stories told are accurate. The food described is accurate. The violin playing is accurate. You can visit or rent Inspiration Hills today for family retreats; information is on the internet.

Chapter 20. We have tried to make every blizzard reference factual and historical.

Quotation Accreditation:
"Credit to whom Credit is Due"

Song Acknowledgements as far as is known:
Theme Song: "Precious Memories" by J. B. F. Wright,
copyright date unknown.
"When He cometh": words by William Cushing, 1856;
music by George Root, 1866.
"If I Gained the World": words (and tune?) by Anna Olander.

Chapter Headings:
—Unless otherwise stated, all Bible references are from the
King James' Bible—
Chapter 1 Heading: Psalm 127:3
Chapter 2 Heading: Matthew 6:11
Chapter 3 Heading: paraphrase of Philippians 4:6
Chapter 4 Heading: Proverbs 4:7
Chapter 5 Heading: Matthew 7:7
Chapter 6 Heading: I Corinthians 13:13
Chapter 7 Heading: I Corinthians 13:2
Chapter 8 Heading: I Corinthians 12:31
Chapter 9 Heading: Psalm 144:9
Chapter 10 Heading: 1984 Psalter 278 versification of Psalm 103:13
Chapter 11 Heading: Philippians 2:27 (pronouns changed)
Chapter 12 Heading: Matthew 6:20a, 21b
Chapter 13 Heading: Psalm 135:6a, 7b
Chapter 14 Heading: Genesis 9:22
Chapter 15 Heading: Job 1:22
Chapter 16 Heading: I Peter 5:8 (modified)
Chapter 17 Heading: Title of song by Rev. Thomas A. Dorsey
Chapter 18 Heading: "Precious Memories" (above) first line
Chapter 19 Heading: "If I Gained the World" (above) paraphrase
Chapter 20 Heading: Job 38:22

The Upsetting Move

"No! No! I won't go!"

"Katherine, Honey, we don't have a choice," Mama's reasonable voice chided. "This farm doesn't belong to us and the landlord wants it now for his son. It is his farm, not ours. So we have to move."

"But he's a mean own landlord, that's what he is! He shouldn't move us off our farm! We've lived here for ten years now. We've worked and worked and improved the whole farm. Now he wants to take it over again. It's not fair!"

"Child, I know this is the only farm you've ever lived on. It's home to you. But you will see. We can make a home of another farm, too. We will!"

"But it'll mean going to a whole new school! I love my school! I love Miss Sands . . . and all my friends," Katherine sobbed. "Especially Jessie."

"Honey, life is life. We have to do what we have to do.

"And remember," Mama added, "God is in control. Nothing happens by chance. He will turn it for our good. Just believe that."

Katherine knew it was useless to say more. The owner really was a nice man; his son was getting married and he simply needed his farm back now.

She was still heartbroken. She loved every cranny on this farm . . .